CURSED

A SPELLBOUND REGENCY NOVEL

LUCY LEROUX

To Nina,
Happy reading!
xoxo
Lucy Leroux

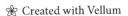 Created with Vellum

DISCLAIMER

TITLES BY LUCY LEROUX

Making Her His, A Singular Obsession, Book One
Available Now
Confiscating Charlie, A Free Singular Obsession Novelette
Book 1.5
Available Now
Calen's Captive, A Singular Obsession, Book Two
Available Now
Stolen Angel, A Singular Obsession, Book Three
Available Now
The Roman's Woman, A Singular Obsession,
Book Four
Available Now
Save Me, A Singular Obsession Novella, Book 4.5
Coming Soon
Take Me, A Singular Obsession Prequel Novella
Available Now
Trick's Trap, A Singular Obsession,
Book Five
Available Now

Peyton's Price, A Singular Obsession,
Book Six
Available Now

The Hex, A Free Spellbound Regency Short
Available Now
Cursed, A Spellbound Regency Novel
Available Now
Black Widow, A Spellbound Regency Novel, Book Two
Available Now
Haunted, A Spellbound Regency Novel, Book Three
Coming Soon

Codename Romeo, Rogues and Rescuers, Book One
Available Now
The Mercenary Next Door, Rogues and Rescuers, Book Two
Coming Soon

Writing As L.B. Gilbert
Discordia, A Free Elementals Story,
Available Now
Fire: The Elementals Book One
Available Now
Air: The Elementals Book Two
Available Now
Water: The Elementals Book Three
Available Now
Earth: The Elementals Book Four
Available Now

Kin Selection, Shifter's Claim, Book One
Available now
Eat You Up, A Shifter's Claim, Book Two
Available now

Tooth and Nail, A Shifter's Claim, Book Three
Coming Soon

Forsaken, Cursed Angel Collection
Available now

CREDITS

Cover Design: Robin Harper
http://www.wickedbydesigncovers.com

Editor: Rainy Kaye
http://www.rainyofthedark.com/

Thank you to all of my readers especially Mary, the Romazing Reader, Andrea Mason, and Karen Shoridge. Special thanks to Jennifer Bergans for her editorial suggestions. Extra special thanks to Alexandre Albore for all of his advice on the Italian aristocracy and help with translations. And finally thanks to my husband for all of his support even though he won't read my sex scenes!

CHAPTER 1

*I*sobel twitched the curtains apart carefully. If she opened them too wide she might be seen. Her room was directly above the center of the drive. A person standing at the right angle could clearly see her curtains. Although, it would have been a little odd if their guests bothered to look in the tiny third-floor window that belonged to her room.

Below her on the expansive gravel drive the staff were unloading the finest traveling carriage she had ever seen. The carriage was a black lacquer monstrosity with red and gold paneling on the doors. The horses that drew it were a sturdy pair of matched greys, doubtless the best that could be had at the last coaching inn their guests stopped at.

A more modest carriage had preceded the one currently in the drive several hours before. It had unloaded a few servants and a multitude of fine trunks. All the servants were male. There were no maids in the group the Garibaldis had brought with them from Santa Fiora, Italy, which meant no women had been included in their party.

The entire household had been buzzing about this visit all week. Guests were rare in this isolated corner of Northumberland. Her employer Sir Clarence Montgomery, a close-fisted minor baronet, did not like to entertain often. But these visitors were an exception. Sir Clarence had mentioned the upcoming visit of his half-sister's husband and son twice in her presence, which for him positively constituted boasting.

Aldo Garibaldi was an Italian count. Miriam Montgomery had met the *Conte* Garibaldi de Santa Fiora at a ball in London during her first London season, shortly after her debut. After a brief courtship, the *Conte* proposed and Miriam went off to Italy for her happily ever after.

Unfortunately for her, ever after was only a decade. She had passed away when Matteo, the count's only heir, was just a boy. According to the servant's gossip, Matteo was a handsome and intelligent young man of eight and twenty, a paragon of propriety and honorable behavior.

He sounded extremely dull.

She didn't know if Sir Clarence had been close with his older sister. There had been a younger sister Anna as well, but Isobel's employer never mentioned her at all. According to the servants, Sir Clarence believed his younger sister had married beneath her. She had died young too, but if Clarence Montgomery felt the loss of either sister with any degree of emotion, it was hidden behind layer upon layer of proper manners and cold British reserve. But Isobel preferred that innate coldness in her employer. It was preferable to the alternative.

She had to leave her last position after the warm and fatherly Sir Isaac Warton, her former employer, made it clear that her duties went beyond the instruction of his spoiled children. He would wait until his wife was away paying calls in the neighborhood to waylay her and flirt shamelessly. Isobel had rebuffed with a polite but firm hand. When that didn't deter him, she had advertised for a new position. She had been fortunate enough to find one right away. She was gone in a few weeks.

Isobel considered herself lucky to have found the Montgomery's. They didn't hold her Scottish heritage against her—although it was probably an excuse for paying her less than the last tutor despite her mastery of mathematics, Latin, Greek, and Italian. Her new charges, Martin and Amelia, were quiet and well behaved. Most importantly, the Montgomerys kept to themselves. Truthfully it was a little dull, but a governess' lot was often this way. Those of her brethren who yearned for adventure and excitement were the ones who got into trouble, something Isobel scrupulously avoided.

She didn't have anyone to talk to outside of her brief interactions with the servants. Her place in the household was in a strange nether position. By birth, she was above the servants, technically equal to the Montgomerys, but circumstances had placed her actual existence below them—far below.

It was a lonely life, but one Isobel had no wish to change. A friend may have inspired confidences she could not afford to share. It was better this way.

Sighing, she turned her attention back to the drive. Where were the *Conte* and his son? She had been watching for several minutes and so far no one had emerged from inside the massive conveyance.

Isobel was contemplating giving up and going to bed when there was a flurry of sudden activity. The occupants of the carriage had finally deigned to leave it to face the dark grey Northumberland sky. Two of the male servants that had been deposited earlier hurried to the carriage to assist a slow moving figure.

Finally. She leaned closer to the window for a better look, her loose auburn hair falling forward. The gap between the curtains widened despite her best intentions to leave them as they were.

No one had mentioned that the *Conte* was an invalid, but there he was being helped down by the servants. He was quickly followed by another man.

Wait.

The figure being helped down from the carriage wasn't grey-haired like the one in the fine waistcoat next to him. It was a young man, moving with painful slowness. The two male servants were positioned at his sides, supporting his weight as they made their way to the front door where Sir Clarence was waiting. Isobel leaned back from the window as the group disappeared inside.

How sad. The count's heir was obviously in very poor health. And it was unmistakably the younger of their two guests. Though he had moved with careful precision, the figure being assisted through the Montgomery's front door had to have been Matteo Garibaldi. He was still fit, with broad shoulders and dark midnight hair. Whereas the *Conte* Santa Fiora had gone grey and had a discernible roundness about the middle.

Why would they come all this way with an invalid?

The Garibaldis had traveled weeks and weeks to reach this cold and rainy corner of England. But wouldn't the warm and sunny climate of Italy have suited an invalid's delicate constitution better? Especially with winter fast approaching.

Perhaps the illness was recent.

There was little point in speculating, Isobel told herself firmly as she climbed into bed. It was late and her days were full. No doubt the servants would have gleaned all the information about their guests by morning.

Between the upstairs maids, the grooms, and the kitchen staff there were no secrets in the Montgomery household. It was an efficient machine for gossip, one wasted on a completely respectable and slightly dull family. But now the servants finally had something to talk about. Her curiosity would be satisfied tomorrow.

CHAPTER 2

The next day, Isobel woke early. As soon as the sun had broken through her windows she was dressed, preparing to get her charges up and fed so they could have their first lesson out of doors. She wanted to take advantage of the fine morning to give her pupils a biology lesson before all the leaves fell from the trees.

Breakfast in the servants hall was full of empty gossip. Very few of the staff had glimpsed their guests since the Garibaldis had arrived so late. But the day was still young, she thought quickly drinking her tea and rushing to join the children.

A few hours later, Isobel was making excuses not to go back inside. The fine weather had lasted beyond her intended lesson, so she and the children lingered going over their readers outside on the lawn near the edge of the woods.

"Ms. Sterling, can we go to the stables, please?" Martin piped up from the blanket where they sat, interrupting the recitation he had been making at Isobel's instruction. "I'd like to show Amelia my pony."

Little Amelia, the Montgomery's ward, nodded eagerly, her face filled with anticipation. The children were due inside for lunch soon, but she could hardly say no to the yearning in those big blue eyes.

Amelia had been living with the Montgomery's for only a short time, a few weeks longer than Isobel herself. The little one was still quite timid about voicing her desires and wishes. Isobel didn't want to discourage her from expressing herself, and she often wondered if Amelia had been as timid when her parents were still alive.

"Very well. Once you finish that passage," she said agreeably.

The children smiled at each other, and Isobel marveled yet again at how easy they were to please. She bade Martin to continue with his recitation. As his clear bell-like voice filled the air, she let her mind wander. Martin was a fine reader and rarely made mistakes. But Amelia was still shy and often stumbled over the words. Isobel wanted her to grow more comfortable before she had her read aloud during lessons. Listening to Martin was one way for her to prepare.

Breathing deeply, Isobel leaned back on the blanket and closed her eyes, enjoying the warmth of the sun on her face. With her auburn hair and pale complexion, she had to be careful not to get too much sun or she would freckle. Despite that, she couldn't help enjoying what decent weather they did get here, especially now that the days were growing shorter and shorter.

A prickling sensation at the back of her neck made her eyes fly open. She sat up and looked down at her charges. Martin was still reading diligently, Amelia's eyes trained on him. But someone was watching them. She could feel it. Turning surreptitiously, she caught sight of an upright figure standing on the other end of the lawn near the stables.

The observer was a dark-haired young man, tall and fit. He was elegantly dressed in a fine gold waistcoat and dark riding coat paired with fawn colored buckskins. His top boots had brown uppers, the gleam of their polish evident even from a distance. And he was staring fixedly at her, not the children.

Isobel's breath caught. She could feel the stranger's gaze as if it was a physical thing, pressing in on her until her heart raced in response. She stifled a wild impulse to jump to her feet and run away into the woods. But instinct told her that would have been a grave mistake.

He would hunt her down.

What was wrong with her? The man was just looking at her. There was nothing threatening about that. From this distance she couldn't be sure of his expression, but it looked benign. He was probably simply wondering who she was.

You are being ridiculous.

After what seemed like an interminably long time the elegant man inclined his head. She was debating on returning his greeting when he turned on his heel and disappeared into the stables.

Was that the count's son?

She couldn't think of who else it could be...but the stranger was no invalid. He had stood without aid and walked with determined steps into the stable.

Confused and unsettled, Isobel changed her mind about a visit to see Martin's pony just now. She would take the children to the stables after lunch, once she was sure their guest was gone.

AMELIA'S EYES shined as Martin proudly demonstrated his little chestnut's many virtues. The girl hung on his every word, their heads were close together in conversation. She reached out to pet the horse that John, the head groom, had brought out for their inspection. He in turn watched Isobel, trying to catch her eye. She pretended not to notice.

"Can Amelia ride him, Miss?" Martin asked hopefully.

The little smile she'd been wearing fell away.

"I'm afraid not," she said. "Amelia doesn't have a saddle."

"She can use mine," Martin said.

Isobel shook her head. "Amelia can't use your saddle because she can't ride astride. Young ladies need a sidesaddle," she said, trying to sound firm.

Amelia looked crestfallen, and Isobel was flooded with guilt. She clearly remembered all the times she'd ridden without a saddle at all, back when her father had been alive. He'd been a mischievous sort, who'd turned a deaf ear whenever her mother had complained about letting their only child run wild, cavorting in the woods and riding astride with him on his horse. The fact she'd been wearing the stable-

7

boy's breeches at the time was a secret her father had taken to his grave.

Stirring from his position leaning on one of the stall doors John leaned forward. "It's all right, Ms. Sterling. Little Amelia's saddle arrived earlier this week."

"Her saddle?" Isobel asked blankly.

"Yes, Miss," John said, nodding at the stable boy who ran to fetch the saddle. John leaned closer while the children began to whisper excitedly. "It *is* her saddle," he added in a low voice. "She used to have a pony too, but Sir Clarence said it was too expensive to keep."

Isobel suppressed a frown and nodded. She had heard the rumors from the other servants when she had started her position. The only reason Clarence Montgomery had taken in Amelia, the daughter of a distant cousin, was because she was an heiress. Though her father had been in trade and the head of the household disdained all those who had to work for a living, the fortune Amelia was to inherit someday had apparently been sufficient enough inducement for him to take her in.

Unfortunately, Amelia's sizable inheritance did not mean she was treated with any degree of warmth. For the most part, she was ignored the way she would have been if she'd been a poor relation. But Isobel was grateful for Martin, a sweet and conscientious child who was completely unlike his parents. Amelia would always have a friend in him—and possibly a doting husband if Sir Clarence pushed for a match between them.

At least Isobel hoped that was where the baronet's intentions lay. It was the most benign of the possibilities she'd considered for her youngest charge.

"It can't be a long ride, especially as Amelia isn't wearing a habit. We have another lesson upstairs in a quarter hour," Isobel called after the children as John helped little Amelia to the mounting block.

"Master Martin can lead the little Miss around the paddock for a few minutes," John said as he opened the gate for the pair.

She nodded and Amelia beamed at her, a genuine and grateful

smile. The little girl primly adjusted her skirts while Isobel went to stand at the paddock fence, crossing her arms on the top rail.

Martin led the chestnut in a slow circuit inside the fenced off area. John joined her at the fence, smiling broadly.

"Pretty as a picture, aren't they?" he asked warmly.

Isobel nodded but didn't say anything. It would not do to encourage him, and he always stared at her a touch too long when she came to the stables with the children.

"Miss Sterling, I hope you aren't planning on going to walk to the village anytime soon. Or if you do that you not go alone."

Puzzled, Isobel pulled her gaze from the children to meet John's eyes. His normal buoyant and overly familiar manner was gone.

"If your duties require a visit to the village, perhaps you'll let me escort you. You see there's been another."

She raised a brow. "Another what?"

Surprise flickered in his eyes. "Another disappearance. The baker's daughter this time."

Isobel drew herself up and stood straight. "A disappearance? I was not aware there had been a previous one."

John clucked his tongue. "Inside servants are falling down on the job, are they? All too busy talking about the count and his son I expect, but there are two young women missing. It's the most excitement these parts have ever seen. The girl disappeared last night on her way home from visiting a friend. And this one can't possibly be a runaway."

"They thought the first girl ran away?" She had heard something about that. It had been a minor note of gossip in the house since the young lady in question wasn't known in these parts.

He nodded. "I don't know her name. Sarah something. She was from Etal, the little berg on the north side of Ford. Went missing almost a week ago. But most everyone thought she'd run off. She was said to be fast," he added in a lower voice. "Had several fellows she walked with, if you know what I mean. When she disappeared even her parents thought she'd gone off with some man. But now they're not so sure, 'cause this other one can't possibly be a runaway. Lottie, the baker's daughter, was engaged to the blacksmith's son and was happy about the match by all accounts."

Isobel mulled that over. "It's still possible that first girl did run off," she pointed out, crossing her arms. "And perhaps the second one was waylaid by a friend or tried a shortcut in the woods and became lost."

Even as the words left her mouth, she realized she didn't believe them. Young ladies from the village, even those of the lower classes, avoided the woods during this season. They were cold and damp, with few discernible tracks or paths running through. It would be easy to become lost amongst those tall trees. She'd made it a point to learn the few paths well during her half-day off.

And the best hiding places, she thought, recalling her insurance policy deep in the woods. It won't come to that, she assured herself. But Isobel felt better knowing she was prepared.

John gave her a disbelieving glance before shrugging. "Until they turn up, it wouldn't do to walk alone. *If* they turn up."

"I will keep that in mind," she said in an even tone before calling out to the children.

Their leisure time was over.

CHAPTER 3

"They want me to dine with the family?" Isobel asked in disbelief.

She had been preparing for dinner in the kitchen. Though she didn't dine with the staff, she did take her meal in their serving hall, just after they had eaten, but before the family's meal was served in the dining room. Some governesses chose to have a tray sent to their room, but Isobel didn't want the servants to think she was putting on airs. Consequently, they were friendlier to her than they had been to tutors past. They still complained about how high in the instep her predecessor had been.

That regard was evident now as the chambermaid, her face red from a dash up to the third floor, nodded eagerly.

"Yes, Miss," Mary said, her round form almost quivering with excitement. "Sir Clarence bade me to tell ye that yer presence is required at dinner tonight. 'E didn't seem terribly happy about it, truth be told," she finished honestly as she reflexively straightened the bedclothes.

Isobel frowned. "If he's not pleased with the idea, why would he ask me to dine with the family?"

Mary literally hopped up and down. "It was the *Nobile* who asked for ye. Did ye know that's what a count's son is called in Italy miss?" she said, walking over to the wardrobe and rifling through it.

"*Nobile* means nobleman in Italian," Isobel said absently. "The count's son is the *Nobile dei Conti di Santa Fiora*. The family seat is southeast of Florence."

Her stomach was tight and her head was swimming. Why would their guest ask for her?

"And I thought Marchioness was a mouthful," Mary said, wrinkling her nose as she struggled to process the intricacies of addressing the upper classes. "We don't have much time, Miss. Ye best put this on," she said, holding up what passed for Isobel's best dress. "So, when did ye meet his lordship?" she asked eagerly.

"Mm, I believe you can call him Lord Santa Fiora, or simply my lord, as the Montgomerys do. I don't believe the use of courtesy titles is common in Italy as it is here. But I haven't met him. Not yet," she frowned, standing still as Mary fluttered over her, undoing the laces of her plain grey gown.

All of Isobel's dresses were plain, in shades of grey, brown, or blue. The dress Mary had chosen and laid on the bed was in the grey family, but it was a lighter shade with a tinge of blue to it with a slightly more flattering cut than any of the others. It was still a far cry from what was currently being worn in the ballrooms of London.

"'Ow romantic! 'E must 'ave seen ye with the children and asked for ye te join them," Mary said, her round face alight with excitement.

Isobel suppressed a scowl. She did not share Mary's anticipation. She was unprepared for a meal with the family. Although she was the daughter of a gentleman, by the time she was of an age to socialize, her father and mother had been long gone. Isobel was certain her manners were above reproach, but the thought of casually conversing with Italian nobility was beyond her. She already knew Sir Clarence was not pleased to include her. What if she embarrassed herself?

Or worse, somehow *exposed* herself?

A cold weight settled in the pit of her stomach as Mary helped her out of her dress. Isobel allowed herself to be jerked back and forth as the servant did up the laces of her stays.

"Not too tight," she said.

If she was laced too tight when she was already feeling light-headed, there was a real possibility she would disgrace herself by passing out.

Mary nodded and laced her loosely. "Good thing for ye, yer waist is already tiny," she said, moving to pick up the grey dress before casting an envious glance at Isobel's midsection. "There's no time to redo yer, hair I'm afraid." She pursed her lips at the simple knot of auburn hair on Isobel's head before she slipped the light grey dress over her and fastened it.

"It will have to do. Thank you," Isobel said, running her damp hands over her waist and smoothing her skirts.

She nodded at the maid and headed down the stairs, trying to calm her racing heart the whole way.

ISOBEL WAS LATE. When she entered the drawing room, it was already full. Sir Clarence and Lady Montgomery were conversing with their guests. In addition to the *Conte* and his son, the minister and his wife were present.

Sir Clarence looked up at her. "Miss Sterling, finally," he said shortly, gesturing for her to join the group.

Isobel stepped closer and curtsied as gracefully as she could. "Forgive my tardiness. I wasn't expecting an invitation to join you for dinner," she said with studied politeness.

If her employer was going to grouse about her lateness, he might have given her more than five minutes warning.

The younger Garibaldi cleared his throat.

An ill-disguised flicker of irritation passed over Clarence Montgomery's face. "Hmm, yes. Allow me to formally introduce Aldo Garibaldi, *Conte* Santa Fiora, and his son Matteo, Lord Santa Fiora. You already know Mr. and Mrs. Sanderson."

Isobel murmured a polite greeting and executed another curtsy for their noble guests. When she raised her eyes, she found the young lord

13

staring at her intently.

"It is a pleasure to meet you, Miss Sterling," he said in softly accented English.

His voice was deep and rich, and more melodious than those of her adopted countrymen. It rippled down her spine in a little wave that she did her best to ignore.

"Thank you, my lord," she said self-consciously, before turning to the other guests.

"Please, call me Matteo."

At her right, Mrs. Sanderson, the minister's wife, briefly widened her eyes at her. Isobel was shocked too, although she nodded noncommittally. Clearly, Italians were clearly far more informal than the English. She surreptitiously checked the Conte's reaction, but he was busy looking down his nose at her drab gown.

Well, there's no helping that now, Isobel told herself sternly. "I trust you have recovered from your long voyage, your lordship."

"Sufficiently," the *Conte* answered shortly. He said nothing more, and her discomfort doubled.

"Well, that's enough idle chatter," Sir Clarence said with a fake jovial grin. "Shall we make our way to the dining room?"

The others agreed with a soft burble of conversation, but it ceased abruptly when Matteo stepped closer to her and offered his arm.

"Allow me to escort you, Miss Sterling."

Isobel paused and threw the others a searching glance. The young lord was breaking the rules of precedence with his offer.

The minister looked disapproving, as did the *Conte* and Sir Clarence. Lady Montgomery wore her perpetually vague expression. Only Mrs. Sanderson looked pleased, a hint of an amused smile on her face.

Uncertainty flooded Isobel. She couldn't very well refuse, could she? How would that look? With a stiff smile, she gave Matteo her arm and they followed the others into dinner.

The situation didn't improve over the meal. Lady Montgomery had seated the party according to rank, so Isobel was at the other end of the table from Matteo, too far for conversation. But that didn't stop him from staring at her throughout the meal. And because he did, everyone else did too.

She could feel the weight of the *Conte* and Sir Clarence's displeasure, but there was little she could do about it. She focused on Mrs. Sanderson, who was seated next to her, asking her about her local charity work while concentrating on swallowing her meal without dropping her fork or spilling her drink.

Almost a decade younger than her dour husband, Beatrice Sanderson occupied herself with good works in the neighborhood, which also gave her a great opportunity to indulge in her favorite pastime, gossip.

At one point in the meal, Sir Clarence succeeded in claiming Matteo's attention with a discussion on the local hunting.

Mrs. Sanderson took advantage of the opportunity to lean in and whisper under the guise of drinking wine with her, "You've been busy, I see."

Flushing at the unspoken assumption that she had done something to attract the young lord's attention, Isobel gave her a surreptitious shake of her head while sipping her own glass. She had always liked Mrs. Sanderson and lying to a minister's wife didn't sit right with her.

She pasted a fake smile on her face and spoke from between her teeth. "I haven't actually. I'm not sure what's going on. You just witnessed my first meeting with our illustrious guests."

Mrs. Sanderson's smile became fixed as well. "Oh, that is interesting," she said in a low voice.

She looked over at Matteo, who had resumed his study of Isobel until his father spoke to him again. Once his eyes were averted Mrs. Sanderson leaned in. "I would not wish to discourage you should this be a beneficial...er, interest, but I would advise caution."

Isobel nodded and smiled in response, uncomfortably aware of the Montgomerys disapproving glances before she changed the subject to the weather.

After what seemed like an interminable amount of time, dinner finally ended. She and the other ladies withdrew to the parlor while the men stayed behind to enjoy their port. Isobel gave silent thanks to the observation of this particular ritual as it gave her the chance to escape from the Garibaldis' collective scrutiny. After a few minutes of conversation with the ladies she excused herself, pleading a headache.

Though she did have the beginnings of a headache, Isobel was most concerned with getting away before the men rejoined the women. It was obvious neither the *Conte* nor her employer approved of the young lord's interest in her.

She reached the second-floor landing with a sigh of relief. Inching carefully down the dimly lit hallway in her long skirts, she felt a hand on her arm and nearly jumped out of her skin.

"Forgive me, *signorina*," Matteo Garibaldi said in his dark velvety accent. "I did not mean to frighten you."

Isobel stared at him with wide eyes. "My lord! How did you come up behind me without me hearing you?"

She didn't understand. With his tall muscular frame, she should have heard something: the sound of his footsteps on the stairs or a creak of the floorboards. But there had been nothing, she was sure of it.

Matteo shrugged and smiled. "I walk quietly. Again, my apologies for surprising you. I had hoped to be able to speak with you more. Perhaps you would join me in a stroll in the garden tomorrow?"

For a moment, Isobel was truly flattered. There had never been any young men in her life, none that admired her near her own station. And Matteo was well-built and handsome with elegant manners.

But there was something in his voice, an unnatural intensity, that didn't match his simple request. His eyes rested on her like dark pools in the dim light, and Isobel's heart picked up speed.

"Er, I'm sorry, my lord," she said eventually. Her throat was tight, but she made herself say the words anyway. "I'm afraid that would not be appropriate."

For a long moment he did not respond. The air filled with a tension that, to her overheated imagination, felt menacing. And it was affecting her vision. It was as if his eyes were gathering the shadows in the hall, pooling and growing blacker before her eyes.

Instinctively she stepped away but he stopped her with a hand on her shoulder. "I understand," he said. "Perhaps you'll change your mind later," he added in a low tone before bowing and walking away.

Feet fixed to the floor, Isobel watched him leave. Once he was out of sight, she took a deep breath and hurried to her room. She readied herself for bed, climbing in and pulling the blanket up to her chin...but sleep was long in coming that night.

~

FIGHTING WITH ALL HER STRENGTH, Isobel pushed Matteo away from her. The resulting cold was startling. Her eyes flew open.

She was in her bed alone. It had been a dream. A nightmare, to be precise.

Taking a shaky breath, Isobel sat up. It was still dark. In her addled dream-state, she'd pushed the blankets and pillow to the floor. Leaning over, she picked them up, hoping that she hadn't cried out in her sleep. Though they weren't next door, there were other servants asleep on this floor. If one of them had heard her, she would be mortified.

Drawing the blanket over her head, she shut her eyes determinedly, but after that nightmare there was no chance sleep would return. Instead, she lay quietly thinking. What if her dream was trying to tell her something?

She had never had a prophetic one before, but her maternal grandmother, Helen, used to have them sometimes. And that dream had been so intense, it didn't feel normal.

Her grandmother used to say that her dreams of the future were of little use as they were confusing, their meaning often murky and unclear until the things they depicted had come to pass.

Pulling the cover tighter, Isobel shuddered. Her dream had started just as tonight had ended, with Matteo coming after her in the hallway. But it hadn't been him at all. What she'd seen in her dream had not been a man. Instead it was a mask, a shell covering something dark—a creature of shade and shadow. Not human.

The realization settled into her heart as her long suppressed instincts flared to life. Something was wrong with the count's son. The gathering shadows she'd seen in his eyes earlier were not some trick of the light.

It was black magic. And of all people, she would know.

How could this have happened? The Montgomery household, indeed all of England, was supposed to be her haven. She had left all memories of magic and spellcraft behind in Highlands. What was left of that life, of her legacy, was buried with her grandmother. And then there was her vow.

She had promised her mother on her deathbed that she would never again do magic, and wouldn't consort with others who did. She had sworn to go to her grave a normal woman.

For a time, when she was quite small, Isobel had embraced everything magical. Her grandmother had been adamant that she be trained in her craft, as had her own mother and grandmother before her. One of her daughter's, Isobel's aunt Moira, had also been trained.

But Isobel's mother had not wanted that life for herself. She always said one witch in the family was enough, and two was already too many. But she hadn't objected when grandmother Helen had decided to teach Isobel magic. Not until Moira had died.

Every other day from the time Isobel was six until she was twelve years old, she would spend afternoons with her grandmother. While her father took care of her classical education, grandmother Helen would teach her about herb lore and basics of spellcraft. They would tramp through the woods near their home, collecting herbs, rocks, and occasional insects or small animals.

Isobel had never learned what actually happened to those small animals. At the time, she had been dying of curiosity, eager to learn the upper-level spells that required such a sacrifice. Growing up around farm animals had taught her not to be sentimental about such creatures. But her grandmother had told her she would learn what was needed at the right time.

But that time hadn't come. Her aunt had died and all lessons had ceased. Her grandmother had been so upset, but even Isobel's father had agreed that it was for the best in light of what had happened.

From that day, Isobel had been taught to fear her gift and what might happen to her if others learned of it. And judging from the way the local villagers had turned on her grandmother, she was right to do so. Even Isobel, a mere child, hadn't been immune to their nasty looks and the whispers that followed her whenever she went into the village.

She clutched the pillow tighter as pain filled her chest. She fought to push the hurtful memories away, but last night's meal had brought all those long buried feelings back to the surface.

What was she going to do about Matteo?

In reality there was little she could do, save avoid him. She hoped he let her.

CHAPTER 4

*I*t was another unseasonably fine day, and Isobel couldn't stop herself from taking the children out of doors. But she quickly came to regret that decision when she felt the weight of *his* stare on the back of her neck.

Isobel resolutely kept her eyes on the children, but Amelia, more attuned to the moods of the adults around her, seemed to sense her tension, She would sneak glances behind Isobel and fidget with her skirts. Isobel tried to reassure the child by smiling at her as their reading lesson continued.

The little girl wasn't fooled. Amelia didn't smile back and her eyes kept wandering behind Isobel to the tree line at the start of the forest. Isobel didn't need to look behind her to know that Matteo was there. She didn't know what he was doing, but she could feel him. She could feel him everywhere these days.

It had been a mistake to bring the children outside again. She should have stayed in the schoolroom for today's lesson, but she'd felt trapped inside the house. If Matteo was nearby—and it didn't matter where—then she knew exactly where he was. It was only out of doors that she could catch her breath lately.

Eventually, Amelia relaxed and Isobel followed suit. Matteo had finally wandered to the stables. Unfortunately, it wasn't the only time they saw him that day. He was strolling the kitchen gardens when the children sat down to lunch and was loitering near the stairs when they went up to the schoolroom to continue afternoon lessons. The pattern was repeated in the following days until Isobel started to feel haunted.

In all that time, Matteo only tried to speak to her once, when she was crossing the foyer after the children to take them upstairs early one afternoon. He appeared out of the shadows with that unnatural quiet step of his, startling her into stopping short when she should have continued after her charges.

"*Signorina,*" he said, bowing deeper than was required for someone of her station. "I see you and the children have been enjoying the fine weather."

Blushing slightly despite herself, Isobel nodded. "It won't last long, I'm afraid," she said, looking around.

She hoped one of the Montgomerys would appear, and even found herself wishing for the count's oppressive and disapproving presence. But she was alone as Martin and Amelia made their way up the stairs and Matteo continued to make polite inquiries, mostly about the children and their lessons, which Isobel felt obliged to answer.

Despite her apprehension, Isobel felt flushed and warm under the young lord's gaze. She avoided looking directly into his eyes, but keeping her focus below his neck just highlighted his broad shoulders and large muscular arms. She idly wondered if Italy had gentleman's sporting clubs like Gentleman Jackson's Pugilism saloon. The width and breadth of his shoulders suggested he spent a lot of time in such pursuits.

Stop.

Matteo wasn't a normal man, and she was not at liberty to enjoy his attentions.

A little movement startled her again, and she looked down to see Amelia creeping close. She smiled down at her charge, marveling at the little girl's bravery. Amelia had shown every sign of being afraid of all adults and Matteo in particular.

The little girl was a more perceptive child than most, and even though Isobel was fairly certain she didn't have the sight, she knew Amelia could feel Isobel's tension every time their guest appeared.

The fact that Amelia had come down the stairs to stand with Isobel said a lot about her inner fortitude. She wondered how much of that was due the untimely death of her parents and being uprooted from the only home she had ever known.

Matteo smiled down at her charge and kneeled down to talk to her. Isobel resisted the urge to pull the child behind her skirts.

"And how do you like your new governess?" he asked softly after a brief discussion on the virtues of ponies, smiling up at Isobel.

That single unguarded look confirmed that the shadowy darkness was still there, flickering behind his eyes. In fact, it seemed like that blackness had spread like a halo around his head.

Amelia was politely answering his questions, but she squeezed Isobel's hand, betraying her discomfort.

"My lord, I really must continue with this afternoon's lessons," Isobel said gently, and Matteo straightened up with a wry grin.

"Of course," he said, shuffling back a few steps.

His movement was slower than it had been a minute earlier and for a second she imagined that a flicker of pain crossed his face. He was definitely growing paler.

"Are you feeling well, my lord?" she asked before she could stop herself.

Matteo nodded, his expression growing distant. "I'm fine," he lied quietly, before walking away.

ISOBEL TOLD herself that she didn't care about what was wrong with Matteo, but his degeneration in the following days was so startling that she couldn't help being concerned.

He stopped wandering the grounds, trailing after her and the children. In fact, she no longer saw him much at all, even when the weather turned poor shortly afterward and they were all confined to the house.

The few times she did see him, he was in such obvious pain that her heart hurt watching him.

He could no longer walk unaided. The male servants that accompanied the *Conte* reappeared, helping Matteo from room to room while the house servants whispered like mad about the turn of events.

"'E was doing so well a few days ago," Mary said with a moue of dismay as she nibbled on some bread, standing near the kitchen hearth.

Isobel, who had come to visit Cook and have a cup of tea, nodded as the matronly woman settled her large frame at the table.

"Aye, but now he's as poorly as when they all arrived," Cook said with a frown. "Must be one of those repeating diseases where the bad spells come and go. Like consumption."

Even though Isobel didn't know of any cases of consumption whose symptoms came and went, she nodded sagely in agreement.

"It's such pity," Mary continued. "'E's such a 'andsome strapping man. I do hope 'e recovers quickly so 'e can enjoy the rest of 'is visit, riding and 'unting with the Master. 'E does seat a horse so well," she gushed.

Cook tsked. "If he does improve, you'd best stay out of his way. Stop peeking at him from behind your lashes. You know very well he only has eyes for one young lady here, one more appropriate to his station."

Isobel blushed as the two women turned to her with knowing grins. "I'm afraid you overstate the case," she said. "His lordship has not expressed an interest beyond seeing me added to the guests for dinner. He is probably just bored and desires to converse with someone nearer his own age. And he's stopped asking for that as well, come to think of it."

Cook scoffed. "Only because he's too unwell to come down to dinner. Takes a tray in his room these days. His interest is as clear as day, or at least it was when he was well. Since he's taken a turn, he's withdrawn a bit but that's pro'lly just because he's ill. Must do something to a man's pride to have his sweetheart see him brought so low."

Isobel's eyes widened in alarm, and she nearly choked on her tea. "I'm not his sweetheart," she said earnestly.

"Not yet," Mary replied in a sing-song voice before continuing to wax poetic on the width and breadth of Matteo's shoulders.

Cook let the foolish maid go on and on, so Isobel hurriedly finished her tea before excusing herself and taking the rear stairs back up to her room.

Things were not going well if even Cook believed Matteo was her sweetheart. If all the servants were of one mind, what were the members of the household thinking? Lady Montgomery probably wasn't concerned, but Sir Clarence and the *Conte* were probably irritated with her right now.

She could only hope that Matteo recovered and this visit ended quickly. She didn't want to jeopardize her position here, and Sir Clarence did not strike her as an understanding person. In truth, if something untoward happened, she was sure the blame would rest on her.

Lost in her thoughts, she was passing the family's private parlor on her way to the third-floor servant stairs. A loud thud inside the room startled her. Alarmed, she hurried to the doorway and saw Matteo, alone, sprawled on the floor. Instinct rushed her to his side. Hovering over him, she was torn between kneeling to help him and running for assistance.

Then he looked up.

His eyes were pitch black, a sharp contrast to his pale face. All the color he had gained in the last week was gone. His face was starkly etched with lines of pain and grief etched on either side of his mouth.

Despite her intention to remain aloof, she dropped to her knees at his side. "Let me help, you my lord."

"No," he said in a thin raspy voice, waving her away.

She ignored him and helped him to his seat with a firm hand. "Should I call the servants? Perhaps find the count's footman? Or the *Conte* himself?"

He shook his head. "Just go," he whispered, squeezing his eyes shut as he put a hand to his chest and winced.

Isobel wanted to wince in empathy too as he rocked back in his seat. Her hand was rising of its own accord to stroke his brow, but the flare-up of black in his aura stopped her short. Heart pounding, she retreated a step and he looked back up at her.

"Leave!" he yelled, making her jump.

She nodded weakly and turned on her heel, nearly crashing into the Conte, who'd appeared out of nowhere. The old man shot her another one of his disapproving stares before dismissing her with an irritated wave. Forced to walk around him, she hurriedly made her way out of the room.

CHAPTER 5

*I*sobel hadn't seen their handsome houseguest for days, but her nights were filled with troubling dreams of him.

She couldn't forget his eyes the last time she'd seen him. Or the pain that had been obvious in his voice. Distracted and still exhausted from lack of sleep, she went down to the kitchen for another cup of tea after morning lessons.

The stable master, John, was visiting the kitchen, as well. He was still wrapped in his thick woolen coat and muffler, sipping on a large steaming cup next to the table where Mary and Sarah, Lady Montgomery's ladies maid, were chattering like magpies.

"Did you hear? Another girl's gone missing!" Sarah said, her wide round face flushed.

Isobel stopped short, half-way to the tea kettle.

"A third has gone missing?" Isobel said, a sinking feeling in her stomach. She took the cup Cook offered her and sat next to the maids with a nod of acknowledgment at John. "Who is it this time?"

John straightened importantly. "A scullery maid for the Hendersons. Janet. Not considered reliable."

The Hendersons were minor country gentry, with a small estate in the neighborhood. They didn't have as large a staff as the Montgomerys, who were the most prominent family in the area. The fact that one of their few maids had gone missing was troubling. Her absence would have been noticed. Even if she had been unreliable.

"What the devil is going on?" Isobel muttered, forgetting herself.

But only Sarah raised her eyebrows. The others just nodded or shrugged in agreement.

John shook his head. "Except for Lottie, the missing women are not the most dependable sort. Might not have been missed under normal circumstances. Makes you wonder."

Isobel silently agreed that the circumstances were suspicious. If someone was luring away young women, perhaps to sell, they would have picked ones just like those who'd gone missing. Except for the baker's daughter, whose disappearance couldn't be explained away so easily.

If a kidnapping ring was operating in the neighborhood, she had to believe they would have been more careful. All of the girls going missing in such a small and relatively isolated area like this simply called too much attention to the disappearances. Hunting young vulnerable women would have been easier in a city.

Unless something else was going on. Throat tight, Isobel forced herself to swallow her tea as the others speculated, sometimes wildly, on the fate of the disappeared. Sarah's idea that the girls had been transported to the Colonies to become courtesans was by far the most entertaining.

But sadly not the most likely, Isobel thought before Mary distracted her.

"I'll be up to 'elp ye dress at quarter to seven Miss," she said.

"To dress? For dinner?"

"Didn't you tell her?" Cook asked, scowling at Sarah. Her features smoothed and she smiled. "You've been asked to join the family for dinner again. It seems his lordship is feeling better. Had a turn last night. Woke up fit as a fiddle this morning, even went riding."

Isobel could feel the color draining from her face. "Is that right?" she asked, breathlessly.

Was it possible?

Of course it was. She'd seen the darkness seeping into Matteo's aura herself. She'd tried to ignore what that had meant, but the unsettled feeling in the pit of her stomach had been there from the moment she had seen him. And her current tension had been a constant companion since she'd learned of the missing baker's daughter.

The coincidence between the missing girl and the man's dramatic recovery was too great. She'd been hoping she was wrong, but she couldn't keep lying to herself. Matteo was responsible for the disappearances.

And if he was, those girls were dead.

"Are you all right?" John was standing in front of her, his hand on her shoulder.

Startled, Isobel suppressed a shudder. "I'm fine," she lied.

Cook pushed John out the way. "You're as pale as a sheet gel. Do you feel ill?"

Isobel took a shaky breath. "Er, yes. I think so. Maybe I've caught Amelia's cold."

The little girl, used to the milder climate of the south, had been suffering from a small cold all week. Isobel never got sick from those sorts of minor complaints, but it was too convenient excuse to ignore.

"That's a pity. Why don't you head upstairs to your bed, and I'll send up a toddy. Maybe you'll feel better in time for dinner," Cook said, as Isobel rose unsteadily from the table.

"I don't think I'm going to be able to dine with the family," Isobel said slowly, "Would one of you please convey my regrets?"

Cook clucked her tongue. "Mary will inform the Master," she said. "It's such a shame, you falling ill just when your suitor is better."

"He's not her suitor," John scowled, and Isobel shot him a grateful smile.

"No, he's not," she agreed before taking her leave.

The children's afternoon lesson was going to be canceled.

∾

Isobel sighed with relief as the dinner hour came and went. No one had questioned her 'illness'.

She'd been in bed since mid-afternoon, truly exhausted in both body and mind. The afternoon's revelation had been difficult to stomach, but she knew the truth now.

But what was she supposed to do? She couldn't stay in bed indefinitely. The Garibaldis were scheduled to stay on for another week at least. How could she look Matteo in the eye and not reveal what she knew about him? How could she look at him at all without screaming?

Maybe it was time for her grandmother to die...again. Surely Sir Clarence wouldn't begrudge her a visit home to bury her grandmother? When he had questioned her about her background, she had been vague about her relations. He would have no idea the woman had passed long ago.

A sick relative probably wouldn't win her any sympathy, but if one had passed away suddenly he would be extremely hardhearted to refuse her leave.

She would have to send herself a letter somehow. If she suddenly received word of a dead relative without getting a missive addressed to her, then there was little hope of getting away *and* keeping her position. The downstairs footman collected the post from the nearby village of Ford every morning. She would need to get down there before he left.

Formulating a plan, Isobel drifted to sleep.

At first, the dream was sensual. She was standing in a darkened room with Matteo, who held her in a passionate embrace. Her body was pressed against his while his long-fingered patrician hands moved over her body. In her fantasy, Matteo was well and whole—and she was enjoying the touch of his gloved hands with an indecent amount of enthusiasm.

But soon the soft caress became hard and threatening. The air in her lungs expelled violently as her chest was compressed with an arm tightening around her like a vise. Gasping for breath, she flailed wildly. Something was shoved into her mouth and covered with something rough.

Certain she was being smothered to death, her eyes flew open as she clutched at the hand on her face. In the darkness of her room, she couldn't make out anything but a large hulking form bent over her.

Terror flooded her body like mercury coursing through her veins. Panicked, she clawed at the hand covering her mouth in order to plead with Matteo for her life.

The realization it was not him came as movement from the shadows caught her attention. The massive hand over her mouth was strong and calloused, the hand of a laborer or a servant.

She tried to scream, but it was muffled by the gag that had been shoved into her mouth as she was hauled out of bed. Lashing out with all her strength, she kicked and screamed anyway, trying to get her assailant to release her.

"Help me. This one's a hellcat," her attacker hissed, and she nearly froze in surprise.

The man had spoken in Italian.

More muffled noises came as the second man stepped from the shadows to join the first, crossing a shaft of moonlight as he did so. He was shorter and thinner than the first and she recognized him as the older servant that served Matteo in his illness. Which meant that the one holding her was the muscular, blunt-featured one.

She doubled her efforts, a terrified whimper escaping her as she fought with all her strength, but it was useless. The second man took hold of her legs while the first held her arms and tied them together. They dragged her to the door and spirited her down the steps of the servant's staircase.

They moved with practiced speed and stealth—a realization that made her heart sink. She doubted anyone had heard her muffled cries for help. Despite her struggles, she was soon out of doors, the cold night air seeping through her thin lawn nightgown with icy fingers. Tears welled in her eyes as she was unceremoniously dumped into the count's waiting carriage and locked inside. The two men climbed onto the driver's box, and the conveyance sped away.

The carriage lantern was unlit and the curtains were drawn. In the dim interior, she could only make out the faint outline of the benches though the moonlight filtering through the covered windows. Isobel tried to sit up, but the violent rocking of the interior and her bound hands made it nearly impossible. Twisting she wormed and crawled until she was sitting up, using her legs to brace herself against the bench. With her hands tied in front of her, she lifted stiff fingers to her mouth to pull at the hastily tied gag.

It took some effort to pull the cloth binding off. Coughing and spitting, she yanked at the gag until it came off in her hands. She couldn't be sure in the darkness, but the object in her hands resembled a man's cravat.

Oh, God.

Was this what had happened to the others? Had they been snatched from their very beds to feed the beast?

In spite of what she knew, it was hard to acknowledge that she was referring to Matteo. Unable to process what was happening, her thoughts skittered over what had transpired to bring her to this point, kidnapped and being taken to him in the dead of night. And her mind threatened to freeze and go dark over what would happen next.

Sweat beading on her lip, she tried to force her hands apart to loosen the rope tying them together. The coarsely woven line bit into the flesh, burning her skin as she desperately attempted to work herself free.

The carriage rumbled to a sudden stop. Isobel was thrown to the floor as the door flew open. The larger of the count's two servants climbed inside and hauled her up with both hands. His fingers dug into her flesh as he dragged her from the carriage.

Taking a deep breath she prepared to scream as loudly as she could, but it died in her throat as she took in the sight before her. The *Conte* and his other servant were waiting in front of a thatched tenant cottage at the far edge of the Montgomery property.

She had passed it in the early days of her employment when she made it her purpose to familiarize herself with the area around her. Back then it had been in a bad state of disrepair, but she knew from the other servants that repairs had commenced hurriedly earlier this month in order to finish before winter truly set in.

But it wasn't the sight of the *Conte* or the cottage that froze her in stupefied shock. No, it was Clarence Montgomery pacing at the edge of the lantern light.

"Sir Clarence!" she gasped as she was hauled in front of the men in her thin nightgown, the large servant holding her in front of him.

Her employer turned to her, anger and a little disgust clearly etched on his face.

"She was supposed to be blindfolded and gagged!" he hissed at the count, his breath steaming in the cold night air.

The *Conte* shot his servants an angry glance before schooling his features. He turned to Sir Clarence. "It hardly matters," he said coldly in his coarsely accented English.

Another blast of icy fear blew through her as the count gestured imperiously and the hulking servant began to drag her to the door.

"No, you can't do this!" she screamed. "I can't just disappear like the others! Everyone is talking about those missing girls. But I'm not an unreliable housemaid or a poor baker's daughter! My father was a gentleman just like you! If *I* disappear in the middle of the night out of my bed, everyone will suspect you!"

Sir Clarence covered his face with his hands before dropping them to glare at the count. "She already knows!" he said nervously. "And if she does then the whole staff does, or will soon."

"It has to be her. He's fixated. Now stop dragging your feet. It's already too late," the *Conte* said, his eyes flat and cold as he looked down at Sir Clarence.

The servant resumed dragging her to the closed door of the cottage. She tried to dig in her heels, but her bare feet grazed the ground as she was hauled unceremoniously to the entrance.

"My lord, think of the children!" she yelled back over her shoulder as the other servant threw open the door.

The dimly lit interior of the cottage seemed more ominous than the mouth of hell. Struggling with what remained of her strength, she twisted her head back in time to see Sir Clarence turning his back on her.

The count, however, followed them inside.

The servant behind the *Conte* entered with the lantern. He hurried inside and set the lantern on a rough wooden table to her left. The light cast the interior of the single room in stark relief.

Little furniture occupied the space. In addition to the table, there was a chair and a fireplace in the process of being retiled. Against the far wall, a mattress lay on the floor. A large and terribly still figure slumped down over it.

It was Matteo, unconscious, with his hands bound behind him.

CHAPTER 6

*I*sobel was too surprised to move, even as she was forced to sit in the lone chair in the room. The man began to tie her wrists to the chair's arms while the other servant faced Matteo and hesitated.

"What is happening?" Isobel asked in a horrified whisper.

This wasn't what she had been expecting at all. Why would Matteo be tied up as well?

The *Conte* ignored her. "Don't dawdle. Untie him," he ordered, before turning to the other guard. "No one opens this door till morning."

Both servants nodded before the shorter one rushed to the bound man. He loosened the ropes until he was able to slip them off. Hurriedly, he adjusted Matteo's arms to a more comfortable position. The movement disturbed the unconscious man and he began to stir.

The sound that came from Matteo as he regained consciousness chilled her to the bone. It was somewhere between a growl and something similar to a cat's purr—an extremely large and dangerous cat like the lion she had heard once at the Edinburgh zoo with her father.

The noise he made sent a shudder through her. And she wasn't alone. The smaller servant straightened up as if Matteo really were a predatory cat that had snapped at him. He backed away quickly. Behind her, the larger servant snickered. Then Matteo opened his eyes and he stopped abruptly.

Isobel took one look at those black soulless orbs and knew she was going to die. Time slowed down for an endless moment, then he blinked and his vision seemed to clear. He looked at her, and for the first time really saw her, bound to the chair not more than ten paces from him.

His face contorted. "No!" His voice was broken—guttural and coarse. "No, not her!"

There was a rush of movement behind her. She didn't have to turn around to know the other men were fleeing. The door slammed shut with the heavy sound a wood thudding against the jamb. It had been barred from the outside, no doubt one of the new "improvements."

"No," Matteo whispered, struggling to his feet.

Isobel closed her eyes and cringed in her seat as he ran toward her. But there was only the whipping of air across her face and then nothing. Opening her eyes she craned her neck to look behind her. He was at the door, banging on it with closed fists. He was crying out, the sound animalistic and desperate. His words were clear enough.

In between repeated shouts of 'Not her!' he was begging his father to kill him.

MATTEO QUIETED down after a few minutes, but Isobel couldn't see him. The door was directly behind her and try as she might, she was unable to twist her neck back far enough. He hadn't moved, but his hard breathing grated in her ears until it evened out and deepened. She wondered if he had fallen asleep. If he had, maybe she could get free.

The servant who had tied her to the chair had rushed through the business, no doubt in an effort to be done before Matteo woke. She didn't want to dwell on that. If the servants, both large and strong men, feared him then what chance did she have?

Trying desperately not to think of what he was going to do to her, she tested her bonds. Even if Matteo was awake, she was going to have to risk it. She couldn't just sit there waiting for the darkness to consume him.

Struggling not to breathe too loudly, she started to tug and slide her arms down and back up. Her already scraped arms burned like someone was setting fire to them, but she didn't stop. She would surely be raw and bleeding by the time she was free. If she got free.

Nearly an hour later, her prediction proved true. The raw skin seemed to burn in contact with the air and a little blood stained the ropes binding her to the chair. Ignoring the pain she prayed the smell of the blood wouldn't remind Matteo of her presence, she worked her right hand free and loosened the left. Grateful her legs weren't tied, she held her breath and stood up as quietly as possible before turning around.

He wasn't asleep. He was sitting on the floor, his back to the door. He stared straight ahead, his face impassive, nearly expressionless. The darkness that stained his aura had grown, almost as if a halo of black smoke surrounded him.

Oh, my God.

Isobel trembled as she instinctively stepped back. A floorboard underneath her creaked loudly and she bit her tongue to keep from swearing aloud. The noise seemed to fill the world, and to her terror Matteo moved his head slightly to look at her. His eyes bored into hers, freezing her to the spot.

Then he smiled—a beautiful and terrible smile.

For one horrifying second, Isobel felt as if she was falling into a dark well as her sanity started to slip away. Catching herself, she jerked abruptly and flew to the other side of the room, as far from Matteo as she could get.

Isobel scrambled into the corner, her arm stinging from something she struck on the way. Turning to face the room, she was dismayed to see the lantern she'd knocked to the ground lying a few feet away.

"No!" she gasped as the light flickered and began to dim.

The glass hadn't broken, but the oil in the bottom had spilled all over the floor. She didn't want to be locked in here with Matteo in the dark. Throat tight, she scrambled forward before all of the lamp's fuel leaked out.

Her hand had just touched the overturned lamp when a larger darker one took hold of it and lifted it off the ground. Moving like lightning, Isobel crawled back and pressed herself against the wall. Matteo, or the thing that was living inside him, lifted the lamp and turned it down to a low flame.

The light dimmed to a faint glow. Unable to look away, she raised her eyes. His head wreathed in shadows, Matteo loomed over her.

A strange grating and rhythmic sound filled the air. It was her lungs fighting to draw air in short labored pants. But her effort failed as soon as he moved.

It was like a snake striking. One second she was curled in a ball against the wall, and the next she had been hauled off her feet and suspended inches off the ground.

The shadows ceased to matter. His face was just inches away, allowing her to see him clearly. Except it wasn't his face anymore. It was a beautiful shell, one made terrible in its absence of a human soul.

However, it wasn't an empty shell. Something was there looking back at her through his eyes—a dark and demonic force. A tremor ran through her entire body as she took in the expression in those eyes. There was an intelligence there and...hunger.

Isobel recognized that look. Other men had watched her with something similar in their expression. But those were normal human appetites, much paler and weaker than this. She *wasn't* going to die right away.

"Please don't," she whispered.

Matteo didn't respond. She couldn't even tell if he was breathing or not. By rights, his respiration should have been as labored as hers. She wasn't a large woman, but no normal man should have been able to hold her like this without showing signs of strain. But he didn't. He just cocked his head at her, the movement eerily reminiscent of a praying mantis.

She was set down on her feet as he pressed a kiss to her forehead.

His mouth was open, his tongue out to taste her. Isobel tried to break free, but his grip was like iron. She sobbed aloud as her feet sliding and dragging across the floor in an effort to get away.

Matteo made that odd growling sound again, and he dragged them a few paces to the right. He pulled at her hair until she lost her footing and fell backwards, his heavy body following her down. Isobel landed on the bed in the corner, pressed into the soft mattress by his weight. She screamed, a cry that was cut short when he forced his face to hers and plunged his tongue into her mouth.

Twisting her head aside with a wrenching motion, she struggled against him, pushing and shoving with her arms and legs. When he tried to kiss her again, she bit him. He withdrew his head once more, laughing at her with a strangely flat parody of Matteo's voice.

His hands were everywhere. One stroked her hip while the other pulled up the hem of her nightgown to stroke the bare skin of her calf and thigh. She used all her strength against him, scratching and biting, but the struggle only helped him. Her attempts to kick him only made it easier for him to slip between her flailing legs. She gasped as his iron hard shaft pressed against her most intimate place.

Matteo's shirt was open now, the skin of his chest abrading her breasts through the thin nightgown. To her shame, her body quickened underneath him. Confused and frightened she clawed at his face, but he easily subdued her before she could do any serious damage. He took hold of her arms and moved upwards, rubbing his whole body against her with another of those strange growling purrs.

She should have felt hot, smothered by his heat. Instead Isobel was chilled to the bone, all of her warmth leaching out as it came into contact with the icy exterior of his body.

When he let go of her to tear at the fastenings of his breeches, Isobel put her arms on his chest and pushed—but this time didn't use her arms.

She used her mind.

Acting on instinct alone she reached out with her ability, terrified that the long dormant skill would fail her. But the power came, raw and unfiltered by a spell to give it form or purpose.

She didn't have the words or knowledge to put Matteo to sleep or kill him. All she could do was push her energy in his direction in an effort to force him away from her.

Her hands ached as they made contact with Matteo's chest. Above her, he convulsed, the blackness in his eyes flaring brightly for an instant. His hands reached out to clutch at her. They bit into her skin, and his mouth opened wide in a soundless scream. Horrified, Isobel desperately gathered her energy back to her body to try and strike at him again, but the blackness in his aura followed it, sticking to it like tar.

Panicked that the creature was now trying to invade her soul, she thrust the energy away again with a force she hadn't known she was capable of.

For the first time in her life, the energy that she'd always associated with her ability left her body. The effort blinded her, burning out her vision with a wall of white. It was excruciatingly painful, like being stung by a bee everywhere.

Eventually the moment passed and her awareness returned in fits and starts. She was weak and out of breath, but otherwise unharmed.

Vision blurred, Isobel gingerly sat up on the bed. Matteo was sprawled on the floor, knocked back by the force of the blast. Her chest was tight and painful as she tried to get a hold of herself. Still trembling, she dragged herself to the end of the bed farthest from the fallen body until she could stand. With unsteady feet, she stepped over Matteo's legs, stopping short at the sight of the stain on the floor a few feet in front of her.

Isobel tried to step around it. But the strange black stain moved toward her like a creeping shadow. Indeed, part of it seemed to be more of an oily shadow than a physical thing—and it was heading right for her, gaining speed as it went.

Gasping, she scrambled back blindly. She fell over Matteo's body and landed on his chest. He didn't move at all as she sprang back up, reaching for the lamp burning low on the nearby table. Jerking to the left, she forced the shadow to adjust its course. Muscles screaming with tension, she waited until the shadow-stain moved over the spilled lantern oil before hurling down the lamp.

Whispering words she'd learned long ago, Isobel used an old fire-starting spell to help build the flames, willing them to form a circle around the shadow. It was one of the first spells her grandmother had ever taught her, one of the few she still remembered.

A terrible sound like tearing metal filled the air as the ring of fire consumed the darkness from the outside in. Covering her ears and pressing against the wall, Isobel watched the oily shadow bubble and boil before the flames suddenly burned out.

An ominous silence fell. The stain on the floor had deepened and it was smoking under the broken glass of the shattered lamp, making her cough. Still pressed against the wall, she shifted to the left, but the blackness didn't follow her.

For a minute she stayed up against the wall. Heart in her throat, she took a tentative step forward, but the stain still didn't track her movement.

Slumping slightly, Isobel relaxed, until she caught sight of Matteo on the floor a few feet away.

Was he dead now?

Isobel inched toward him until she was close enough to touch him. She reached out to prod him with her foot. He didn't move. Kneeling down, she put two fingers on his neck, feeling for the beat of his heart.

His heartbeat was strong and steady, and he was warm, almost burning hot in the relatively cold room. She hadn't been imagining that when she'd fallen on top of him. And this close she could feel his breath against her wrist. Had it been the shadow that had made him so cold earlier? Had she destroyed it?

Had she...saved him?

Pushing away that hopeful thought, she stood up. She didn't know what had happened. And all she knew was that the shade inside him wasn't in control now.

What was going to happen when he woke up?

A memory of those hungry and watchful black eyes came, and she squeezed her own shut to blot out the image. The effort failed.

Instead, her mind threw up other nightmare scenarios—body after body of all of those women who had preceded her.

Raising a shaky hand to her lip, she glanced at the rumpled bed. There was a pillow lying on it and Matteo was unconscious...completely vulnerable on the floor.

A tremor ran through her and tears began to stream down her face. It was impossible. Not only would she be signing her own death warrant when the *Conte* opened the door in the morning, but she simply couldn't bring herself to hurt Matteo, despite what he'd been about to do to her. And for all she knew, she had permanently damaged him. He might even be dead by morning.

She tried to tell herself she shouldn't care, but her whole body flooded with remorse.

Stop that.

Isobel needed to worry about herself. Sucking in a deep breath, she spun around, taking stock of the room. It was fairly dark inside the cottage now that the lantern was gone, but she'd always had good vision in the dark. Her grandmother used to tell her it was a practitioner's natural element, a fact she was grateful to now.

Her examination didn't show much. There was little outside of what she'd glimpsed earlier. The furniture was sparse and there were no convenient weapons lying around. The windows were high and small. She could have fit through one, but she had heard the *Conte* order his servants to guard the door till morning. They would be on her before she hit the ground.

A pile of brown at the far corner of the mattress attracted her attention. Pulling it off, she found it was Matteo's caped greatcoat. Riffling through it, she found the pockets empty. Disappointed, but not surprised, she dropped it on the bed before thinking better of it. The room was cold enough to see her own breath, which meant it would be freezing outside. If she discovered a way out, she would need the protection the coat offered. However, there was little she could do for her bare feet, she thought, looking down in dismay.

A nearby roll of thunder distracted her from her self-pity. It was accompanied by the distinctive patter of rain on glass. Her heart sank. A storm would make any escape much more difficult.

Unless the guards decide to take shelter from the rain.

If they did, maybe she could slip away. There was no way for them to know that she had survived. As long as the door was left secured then maybe she had a chance.

Isobel looked down at her feet again. She had to do something. If she had the protection of Matteo's coat, then maybe she could tear strips off her nightgown to wrap around her feet. It was already torn from their earlier struggle. Wincing at the memory, Isobel fisted her hands and sucked in a steadying breath. She turned to Matteo with a critical eye. His exposed chest moved up and down steadily, his lower half still covered in his breeches and boots.

Still alive. Her life, on the other hand, was in a far more precarious position even if she managed to get out of the cottage unseen.

Do whatever it takes.

She needed to be mercenary to survive. Steeling her resolve, she walked over to Matteo's prone form and kneeled down. Tentatively, she reached out and took hold of one of his boots, tugging gently. It was harder to remove than she'd thought. By the time the boot slipped, off she was sweating and shaking, terrified that he would wake up. But he didn't stir. She worked off the second boot and examined them both.

Stepping into the boots and trying to walk proved impossible. They were simply too large. Isobel almost fell over twice before giving up. Dashing away the moisture that stung her eyes with the back of her hand, she put the boots down next to Matteo. His thick woolen socks would have to suffice. Slipping those off much more easily, she drew them over her feet and was grateful for their warmth. She cast another guilty glance at Matteo before dragging the blanket off the bed and throwing it over him. Then she took it off and put it back on the bed.

She would *not* help him.

Trying to move quietly in case the guards were still outside despite the rain, she carried the chair under the far window. Unfortunately, the blasted thing seemed to be swollen shut. Hands scrabbling on the wood she tried the other window. It too was damaged, and no matter how hard she tried, she couldn't open it. Were they nailed shut?

Giving way to self-pity, Isobel sat on the floor, her eyes stinging. Her eyes swung from the sealed windows to the door, trying to formulate a plan. But no brilliant ideas came to her. Defeated, she sat there for a few minutes, trying to prepare for the worst.

Though she wasn't a brave woman, it was harder than she'd ever imagined to sit there and meekly accept her fate. Giving up simply wasn't in her nature.

Gathering her knees to her and hugging them tightly, she pushed away her feelings of despair and helplessness. She would do something—even if it meant attacking the guards the minute they opened the door in the morning. She couldn't possibly win, but at least she would go down fighting.

It took her some time to realize that the sound of drops she heard were not from her tears falling on the floor.

The roof was leaking. On the other side of the newly installed chimney was a small puddle. A desperate idea came to her. It wasn't likely to work, but she had to try.

Pulling the table with effort, she positioned it directly over the puddle. Then she put the chair on top of the table before adjusting Matteo's coat over her shoulders. She tied the ends together to keep it from dragging and tripping her before climbing onto the chair. Bent over nearly double, she pushed at the weak spot in the thatched ceiling. With some determined pushing, she could poke her finger out to feel the rain and night air outside. But getting her whole body out this way would require some effort.

Wasn't there something her grandmother had taught her that would help? Some spell for moving immovable objects? If there was, she couldn't remember it. The fire starting spell wouldn't help much, either. Even if the damp thatch caught, the smoke would alert people for miles around.

Doesn't matter.

Spine stiffening, Isobel continued to tear and poke at the weak spot in the roof. Eventually, she had created a hole large enough to fit her head through. The rain was slowing down. The occasional fat drop pelted her face, running down her neck and chest to chill her despite the stolen coat.

She tried to widen the hole with her shoulders, but all she succeeded in doing was scratching her neck. Crouching down again, she carefully pulled the coat over her head, holding on to the nearest beam of wood in the roof to keep her balance. Then she forced upwards with her back, using all her strength. A loud crack sounded as one of the supporting branches gave way and her shoulders were able to rise above the gap she'd opened wide.

Hoping the noise of breaking wood was covered by the wind, she crawled upwards. She hauled herself through the hole, sucking in a deep breath as the branches and bundled thatch scraped her sides. Without the protection of the great coat she would have been torn to shreds. As it was, she would probably be bruised from neck to knee.

Finally, she was outside in the damp night air, clinging to the thatch as she sagged there, trying to gather her strength. Repeatedly adjusting the coat, she crawled to the edge of the roof and looked down. The ground seemed very far away.

There was no convenient tree to climb down, but there was a pile of canvas-covered building materials directly under the eave of the house. Praying that it was more thatch and not lumber and nails, she crawled over the edge, dangling in the air for an endless moment. The she let go.

She hit the canvas pile with a thump. Though her hope that it was more thatch was probably correct, it didn't really matter since it felt like she had landed on a pile of lumber. Testing each limb gingerly, she gave thanks that at least all her bones appeared to be intact. Grimacing, she moved off the pile, stepping carefully on the muddy ground. She made her way to the side of the house.

Holding her breath, she peeked around the corner. Thankfully there was no sign of either guard. Picking up the hem of the coat, she ran to the shelter of the trees on the left side of the house. She kept running until she was deep in the woods.

CHAPTER 7

espite Isobel's familiarity with the woods, her wild flight in the dark ensured she was lost for nearly an hour. It would have been much longer if she hadn't stumbled on the stream that bisected the woods into northern and southern halves. She followed the stream for nearly a mile before coming to the hollow fallen log where she had hidden her insurance policy.

There were two bags, one filled with clothing and a much smaller one with a few essentials. It was in this second one that she dug into first, pulling out a jar of salve she'd made from one of her grandmother's recipes. Trying to be quick, she spread some on the cuts and scrapes on her arms and neck with numb fingers.

Thankfully, her smash cash hoard was also present. There were ten pounds in notes and coins at the bottom of the sack and an additional twenty sewn into the lining. It represented all of the money she'd earned in her current and former positions as well as the sad remnant of what she'd inherited when her parents died.

For a moment, Isobel bowed her head, the weight of tonight's events pressing down on her.

It's going to be all right.

Her foresight in hiding these things in the woods meant she had a real chance now. Of course, never in her wildest nightmares had she imagined that these would be the circumstances that led to her flight. She'd always imagined an accident would lead to her exposing her abilities, necessitating a swift departure.

Well, in a way some aspects of that fear had come true, she thought, pulling out a black dress and petticoats from the larger bag.

Dressing in the clean drawers, wool stockings, and flannel chemise was a trial in the dark since she'd had to abandon the warmth of the stolen great coat to do so. The icy wind bit into her flesh, slowing her progress as her trembling hands hurriedly donned the rest of her clothing. Yanking an extra pair of her own socks over her feet, she put on the new low leather half boots she'd spent a month's wages on.

At the time, she'd thought them an exorbitant addition to her escape provisions, but now she thanked the impulse that had made her buy them. With one last regretful glance at the greatcoat and muddy socks, she pulled on her hooded cape and gathered her belongings.

Wrapping the stolen items together, she bent low to shove them into the log. It would have been nice to keep the coat longer since it was still raining, but if they pursued her then she wanted to ensure they would have as few possible signs of her direction as possible. And it wasn't like she could take it with her. A woman wearing a man's garment would attract too much attention.

Streaks of light were starting to lighten the sky. Any minute now, the guards would come to collect her body and discover Matteo —*alive?*—on the floor and her gone.

She needed to be as far away from this place as possible.

CHAPTER 8

*M*atteo's head felt like it had been split in half. Disappointment and despair flooded him. It wasn't the headache that disturbed him. He deserved the pain, but feeling it meant he was still alive when by rights, in a just world, he should have been dead.

He didn't want to open his eyes. If he did, he would see what he had done. He wasn't sure what that was. His memories of being the monster were always vague and shadowy. Some days he woke up to himself with no recollection of the night before. But there would be no escaping the reality of what he was when he found the body.

And there was always a body. There was no way he would be here now, aware and conscious-stricken, if there wasn't. He couldn't be himself without death.

If his father loved him, he would let him die. But he was his father's only heir and Aldo Garibaldi never gave up, no matter what the cost. The price didn't matter to his father, but it mattered to him.

He had to find a way to die.

This desperate voyage to England had given him hope for a brief time. There had been a plan and chance for a cure. But days after their arrival had seen those hopes dashed. For a time, he'd ignored the truth and pretended. He lied to himself, crafting a little fantasy over a pair of more green-than-hazel eyes and auburn hair.

A shooting pain in his chest stole the air from his lungs.

Isobel.

A hazy memory of her wide and frightened eyes came back to him.

Oh, God, no!

How could his father have done this to him? It was bad enough waking to a body, but to know that it was *her* was destroying him.

There was no more tomorrow, he thought, tears stinging at his eyes. Despite the horror of the nightmare he was living now, he hadn't cried before. He'd torn out his hair and vomited on more than one occasion, but he hadn't cried. Weeping gutturally on the floor, his pressed his face to the floorboards for a long time.

Get up.

He had to prepare her body. He wasn't going to let his father's men do it. No one would touch his Isabella but him. He'd bury her himself.

And then he would find a knife or a pistol to end this. Finally. Maybe he would catch a glimpse of her in the afterlife on his way to hell.

Stiff from a night on the ground, Matteo opened his eyes and sat up slowly. He braced himself for the sight of Isobel's body, but froze instead.

The cottage was empty. He stood up, spinning around to take in the whole room. No one. Pulling the cover off the bed, he checked to make sure she wasn't hidden there, but thankfully there was nothing.

Had his father already been here? Was he trying to hide what he'd done? Aldo had to know Matteo would never forgive him for choosing Isobel. Had his men spirited her body away while he slept?

He went up to the door, banging on it and shouting—even kicking it a few times before he realized his feet were bare. As usual, he was ignored. The men never opened the door until his father showed his face, and Aldo calmly waited until after his breakfast before making an appearance.

Matteo had managed to crack the old wooden door with his fists by the time it was finally opened.

His father was standing behind his servants, Nino and Ottavio, who kept their distance from the door as they always did when they came to release him after one of his bad spells.

"Where is she?" he bellowed, running forward.

His father opened his eyes wide, taking Matteo's hands to hold him aside while the servants hurried past him. He shook off the restraint and grabbed the lapel of Aldo's coat.

"How could you do that? Why did you have to choose her?" he asked hoarsely.

His father started to roll his eyes before stopping himself. "She was the one you wanted," he said dismissively.

"Not for this! I wanted to court her!"

Aldo suppressed a sneer, but his face was tight. "You know that was impossible, now please stand aside while we clean up here."

Matteo was about to protest that he'd already done that when Ottavio came back outside.

"She's not here."

Shock and surprise froze Matteo to the spot. His father hadn't had Isobel's body removed before he woke. The old man looked just as stunned as he did. Aldo pushed past him, going over to stand next to Nino, who was staring wide-eyed at the hole in the ceiling.

"How can this be?" the *Conte* asked in a low voice.

Matteo staggered back into the cottage and collapsed in the chair, next to the remnants of a broken lamp. He took in the rest of the room once more and looked down at his bare feet.

"She's alive. I'm myself, and she's alive," he rasped.

Isobel had escaped death at his hands last night. Somehow, against all odds, she'd found a way. His missing greatcoat and socks were proof of that. The weather had been bitterly cold the last few nights. She'd taken what she could to protect herself from the elements.

Alive, alive, alive.

He shut his eyes and thanked the god he'd thought had forsaken him.

When he opened his eyes, Ottavio was walking back inside.

"She made it over the roof and into the woods. The tracks

continue some way past the tree line. She must have escaped after the rain had mostly stopped."

"We have to find her. Can you tell what direction she went in?" Aldo asked.

Matteo lifted his head to his father. "Leave her alone," he whispered.

Aldo dismissed him with a wave. "Don't be a fool. We *need* her. She obviously has magic. There's no way she would have gotten out of here without it—not without killing you first. She did what that *puttana* crone was supposed to. Look at yourself. You are whole," he admonished.

Matteo absorbed that in silence. Was it possible? Did his beautiful Isobel have some magical ability? Had she cured him?

No, no. It was too much to hope for. He was a monster, a demon from the pit of hell and those were not dispatched so easily. But he wasn't about to disagree with his father.

"If that's true, Isobel deserves her freedom. Leave her be," he said, refusing to add that *he* would search for her on his own.

He needed to know that she was all right. He had no memory of what he'd done after he saw her face last night. Matteo never remembered what he did during one of his black spells—although he'd seen the strangely pristine bodies the next day.

Aldo scowled. "We can't take the chance. Not only is there the risk that she'll return to make accusations, but there is every possibility that this cure is temporary. Your affliction could return tomorrow for all we know." His father gestured to Ottavio. "Take my son back to the house and then come back with Clarence and his hounds. We'll start searching the woods together."

"No," he said, rising to his feet. "There's no chance I'm leaving."

His father scowled at him. "You need to rest."

Matteo shook his head. "I'm fine. I feel better than I have in months," he said, before finding that it was the honest truth.

It had been so long since he'd felt this clearheaded. There was no pain or weakness, and despite his half-dressed state he actually felt warm.

His father still looked skeptical, but Matteo wasn't about to let him hunt down Isobel like some sort of animal. He wasn't leaving.

Turning to Ottavio, Matteo ordered, "Go fetch me a change of clothes and another coat. I'll be leading the search."

Ottavio looked at his father for confirmation, who nodded impatiently. "Do it and be quick about it. We don't have time to waste."

CHAPTER 9

*M*atteo's Uncle Clarence was beside himself with worry when he found out Isobel had survived the night.

Sir Clarence was all for putting a bullet through her head as soon as they found her, but his father berated him into silence, making it clear that they needed Isobel alive. He finally agreed, but Matteo watched Sir Clarence carefully anyway as they tramped through the muddy forest.

If his uncle was a threat to Isobel, Matteo would do whatever was necessary to protect her. But he felt like a hypocrite for wanting to give his uncle hell, when *he* was the one who'd tried to kill her.

Here and there the dogs caught Isobel's scent, losing it several times in the mud. But they always picked it up again. It was very steady alongside the stream. It had probably been too cold for her to cross it without shoes in order to mask her scent, or she hadn't thought to do so during her flight in the dark.

About a mile away from the cottage, they found the fallen log with his great coat and mud-crusted socks inside.

"What the hell is this?" his father asked with a scowl. "Is she running about in her nightgown?"

Matteo sat on the log and shook his head. "No," he said softly. "This confirms it. She must be a witch."

Sir Clarence swung around to frown at him. "How does this prove that?"

He hung his head and examined the muddy toes of his Hessians. "I made her nervous. She could see me for what I was, and had the foresight to prepare. This must have been where she hid provisions for a quick escape...in case the worst happened."

Well, the worst had befallen her. She'd come within inches of dying at his hands.

The count swore. "If she had a change of clothes, then she could have made it to Ford village or farther. We must go back to the manor house and fetch horses. We will split up and search the local inns. We mustn't let her board a carriage, or we'll be forced to pursue her on the roads."

They set off at once, dividing into teams. Matteo kept close to his uncle in case they did come upon Isobel unawares. They checked the roads and nearby fields while his father and Nino inquired at the inns where the coaches stopped.

"She'll go north to Scotland, not London," Sir Clarence said authoritatively as they rode. "She knows no one in town and has very little resources. If she has any destination in mind, then it's probably some place familiar."

"Do you know where her home is?" Matteo asked.

"No. Some village somewhere in the Highlands. Never caught the name but the other servants might have. I'll have to question them," Sir Clarence said shifting uncomfortably.

"What will you tell them about her disappearance?" he asked.

The baronet shrugged. "That she got a summons from her family. Your father offered his coach to the post road, where she took off on her own."

It wasn't a good excuse, but the servants probably wouldn't question their employer too closely, no matter what they secretly believed.

His father hurried back to them. "The post left at dawn, but there

53

were no passengers taken up here. It's possible she waylaid a private coach further up the road. In any case, there's no sign here," he said.

"Maybe she didn't go inside. Did the ostlers see nothing?" he asked.

"If they did, they're not speaking. We'll have to check the inn at Etal," the *Conte* muttered as he mounted his horse.

Matteo's instincts clamored for attention. "That will take too long. I want to go ahead and try to overtake her on the road. We'll check the nearest border stop," he said, then turned to Sir Clarence. "Which is the closest crossing?"

"The post goes from here to Coldstream, but there's a stage to Norham from Etal too," he said pensively. "But it's not likely she made it to the stage on foot since it leaves early morning. We're more likely to find her at the Rose and Crown in Etal or hiding somewhere nearby."

"Then you stay here while Father goes to Etal. I will go ahead to the border on my own."

His father scowled at him. "Not alone. Take Ottavio."

That was what he'd expected, but it still annoyed him that he was no longer his own man. "Very well. Ottavio let's go."

"Don't let him out of your sight," his father called to the servant.

The bullish young man nodded back at his father, and they took off on the north road.

CHAPTER 10

*M*atteo watched the inn courtyard from an upper story window. He'd berated Ottavio into waiting outside, but it had taken some effort.

His father's servant was growing more and more insolent as time went on. But Matteo had won the argument in the end. They needed more than one pair of eyes on the passing coaches, so the man was watching from the stables.

Of course, it was possible he had chosen incorrectly. They were in Norham, despite the fact the Coldstream post stop had been closer to the manor house. Coldstream was also the most direct route to Edinburgh, and then to the Highlands. From Norham one had to travel to Chimside and then up the circuitous coastal route before getting to Edinburgh. But his instincts said Isobel wouldn't do the expected thing and fly home via the most direct path. She would try and throw them off the scent.

On horseback, they'd traveled much faster than was possible for the stage coach, using paths that were inaccessible by any sort of conveyance. If Isobel was on the road here, she had to be behind them.

Matteo sighed and briefly closed his eyes. There was always the possibility that his uncle had been correct and they'd already captured her before she even had a chance to reach either the post or the stage. It was also possible she was taking shelter around Ford.

His uncle assumed she had no friends in the neighborhood. Sir Clarence had been sure she didn't know anyone outside his household, but Matteo was equally certain there was a lot about his governess that he didn't know.

Turning back his attention to the window, he sipped at the lukewarm tea one of the inn's maids had brought him. He'd wanted coffee, but they didn't have any, and it had been a choice between tea or ale. And he didn't need anything that dulled his senses. So he drank the damn tea.

In the distance, a horn sounded. When another carriage turned into the inn's driveway, he roused himself and sat up straight. The last two had been private traveling carriages. He'd been assured by the innkeeper that the stage was due momentarily, but the bad roads had made "a moment" an eternity.

Several people alighted from the carriage, two men, a matron, and a widow. They hurried inside to relieve themselves or to buy a quick meal. The coach had a timetable and would leave them regardless of their ultimate destination or the fare they had paid.

There was no bright red hair among the passengers that had descended. Disappointed, Matteo went downstairs to make sure all of them had disembarked, pulling on his greatcoat and large brimmed hat as he went.

He bypassed the taproom and went outside, gesturing to Ottavio who'd been watching from the stables, which stood a few feet away. When the servant shook his head, Matteo found the stable master and instructed him to saddle two fresh horses.

Maybe there would be enough time to reach Coldstream, he thought, his heart heavy. Making his way to the taproom to wait, he stood in the corner nearest the door as the passengers hurriedly finished their business and started to head back to the coach.

He was about to join the exodus when he noticed the figure in black again, the woman in widow's garb. She was completely covered in black crepe from head to toe. A heavy veil obscured her face and hair.

At first he wondered how she could see anything past that thick layer of black over her eyes, but a moment later it was her steps that captured his attention. Not only could she see clearly, but she moved with grace. A grace that was as familiar to him as her lovely face.

Isobel.

He almost tripped over a chair in the sweeping rush to get to her before she made it to the doorway. His knee was throbbing as he reached her, but he didn't care. She saw him before he reached her. She froze as he reached out and pulled her into his embrace.

"I'm so sorry," he whispered against her veiled ear as he was engulfed by her familiar scent of flowers with a hint of vanilla. "I'm so sorry."

"Sir, I don't know you," Isobel said loudly, pushing at his chest and arms.

He was almost crying with relief. It was definitely her. She tried to disguise her voice, but he would know her anywhere. He didn't let her go, reaching up to tug the veil off her head.

Isobel's bright auburn hair was mussed as he pressed his face into it, surreptitiously pressing a kiss to her head before pulling away so he could look down at her face.

They stared at each other for a long moment.

She looked so afraid of him, and it broke his heart. His voice was hoarse as he called out the innkeeper, who was watching them with concern.

"My wife and I would like a private parlor to rest," he said, keeping a tight hold on Isobel's arm until she winced and he relaxed his grip.

"Your wife?" The innkeeper's voice showed his confusion.

The widow's weeds contradicted Matteo's words.

He gave the man his most charming smile. "Yes. She's in mourning for my mother," he said in a bored tone.

The English always responded to bored aristocrats. Perhaps the Scotts would, as well.

The innkeeper hesitated before recovering himself. "Right this way."

The man gestured to a door opposite the taproom entrance as the horn sounded for the departing mail coach.

Isobel's face was a picture of distress as Ottavio came in to tell him the horses were ready. The oversized servant stopped short when he saw him holding Isobel in her black dress. Matteo hastily waved him away before hustling her to the parlor.

Trying to be gentle, he led her to a chair before turning to close the doors behind them.

Her beautiful eyes had filled with tears as he sat to her right, in the chair closest to the door in case she decided to bolt. But Isobel seemed to know that there was no escape as she sat there, shoulders slumped. A single tear escaped her eye, and he leaned over to wipe it away before he could think better of it.

She shrank away from his touch, and his chest tightened.

"*Cara*, I never wanted to hurt you. I never wanted you to see me like that." She continued to look down at the table so he reached out to take her hand.

"Please look at me," he pleaded.

Isobel pulled her hands into her lap before taking a deep shuddering breath. When her eyes met his, he felt a painful jolt pass through him.

Her feelings for him were all too clear in those green and gold orbs. Fear, disgust, and maybe even some hate. He didn't blame her. She had every right to revile him. Even if she had helped him, whether she had meant to or not.

"Isabella, is...is it over?"

He couldn't completely crush the hope in that question. It was there in his voice. The expression in Isobel's eyes shifted to one of pity.

She cleared her throat slightly before speaking. "I'm...I don't think so," she said, not pretending to know what he was talking about.

Breathing was a lot harder suddenly. He'd told himself over and over on this journey that his affliction wasn't simply gone, but he had been lying to himself. The hope that he hadn't acknowledged was crushing him now.

"Oh," he said softly.

Next to him, Isobel's beautiful face blurred.

"I still see it. It's not like before, but there is still a trace of something...unnatural in your aura."

That was enough to snap him out of his flood of melancholy.

"What is it you see?"

Isobel looked at him and then down uncomfortably.

"Please, I need to know."

When she remained silent, he decided to speak. "We came to England to seek the advice of a healer, an old crone who lived an hour from my Uncle Clarence's home."

At the mention of her employer Isobel's expression hardened, but he continued.

"My mother used to speak of her when she was alive. Mama called her a *Befana*, an old witch, and said she had rare healing ability and could even cast curses if someone wronged her. My mother was full of such stories. My father ignored them as fancies, but a few months ago he had reason to give them a second thought. He wrote to Clarence to ask if the witch was still alive, and we were so relieved to hear she was. My father brought me seeking a miracle. But after coming all this way, there was no miracle. The crone had died shortly before we got here. I don't even know if the woman had the skill to cure me, or if we were on a fool's errand."

There was silence for a long minute.

"What happened a few months ago?" Isobel asked in a strained voice. "How did this happen?"

Matteo looked at her helplessly. "I'm still not sure. I thought I was ill, something I'd been exposed to in my last voyage. I used to travel quite a bit. My father accused me of having wanderlust and for a time it was true. But I had been home several weeks and then I don't remember what happened. I never do. I only see what I did after and I..."

He trailed off, unsure what to say. His guilt was eating at him like acid.

"You don't remember asking your father to kill you last night?"

His head snapped up. "No, but if I did it wouldn't be the first time I asked. I remember others."

"From the day after?"

Nodding, he looked down at his hands. They seemed much larger than he remembered. Perhaps it was just in contrast to hers.

"I'm my father's only child. His heir..." It was a poor excuse. He should have had the courage to end it himself. "I'm sorry I pretended," he whispered.

Across the table, she shifted in her seat. "What did you pretend?"

"That I was a normal man. When I was around you, it was so easy. I felt fine at the time. That's what happens...after one of my spells. My head clears, and I feel like myself again. Or something like myself. I'm almost not sure how I used to be anymore. All my memories from before don't seem real."

Isobel looked thoughtful now, sympathy sneaking into her expression despite her disgust of him. His heart in his throat, he summoned to courage to ask.

"Isabella, can you fix me?"

Her face fell and so did the fragile hope that had risen in him.

"You did something to me last night. I woke up myself with-out...without having to hurt anyone."

"And that hasn't happened before? Does someone always have to die before you return to yourself?"

He nodded, his throat thick. "Yes. Otherwise I stay that way. I have spent days completely mad, and my father became desperate..."

She absorbed that in silence. "I don't know what I did last night," she whispered eventually.

He looked at her entreatingly. "But you have magic. You can see the evil in me and last night you defeated it."

Isobel's hands twisted on one another. "I told you, I don't know what I did," she said. Her voice had grown slightly shrill. "What happened was chance. I don't have the training. I only know what my grandmother taught me and those lessons stopped very early in my life. *I can't help you.*"

"But you already have," he said desperately. "Can't you just do what you did again? If it comes back, that is..."

Strands of her hair flew into her face as she shook her head violently. "I don't know."

He took hold of her hand. She stiffened, but he held on. "If you had to try, could you? Please?"

Isobel's mouth opened and shut a few times, but the door behind them swung wide before she could reply. Ottavio came in, nodding to him.

"I sent a man on horseback to the *Conte* with a message that the girl has been found," he said in Italian.

Matteo turned, shooting daggers at him. "I didn't tell you to do that."

Ottavio shrugged. "Those were the Conte's orders. He'll join us within the day," he said, giving a shallow bow before taking his leave.

"Your father is coming here?" Isobel gasped, eyes wide in a rapidly paling face.

The impulse to lie was strong, but he couldn't do it. "*Cara*, we can't let you go. You're my only hope. Even if I could release you, he never would. Not after what you did. He'll keep you under lock and key and make you try and try and try."

Her expression could have singed paper. "And if I fail, will he send me to my death again?"

His mouth gaped as he tried to find words to reassure her. "I won't let him hurt you. Not again."

She scoffed, her eyes the only brightness is the dim light. "How are you going to stop him?"

Matteo sat up straighter, his old resolve and sense of determination flooding him.

He had missed feeling this way, and he wouldn't be if it wasn't for Isobel. It was her gift to him and he would use it to protect her however he could.

"I'll find a way."

CHAPTER 11

The weather had improved by mid-afternoon. Feeling claustrophobic in the private parlor, Isobel asked Matteo if they could walk around the village to get some fresh air. They'd walked past the small rows of buildings that comprised of the town center, to the lanes that ran alongside the fields when Matteo complimented her on her disguise.

Trying her best to ignore the large servant trailing them, she turned her attention to his comment. "My grandmother always said widows had the greatest freedom in society. She wore black my whole life, long after my grandfather passed."

"As a disguise, it was a stroke of brilliance."

"Not precisely. You still recognized me somehow."

He smiled briefly, and she was ashamed at the sudden warmth that flooded her chest despite the chill in the air.

"I know the way you move."

Isobel flushed. It was a terribly intimate thing to say. She didn't even try to come up with a response, but one was unnecessary.

"How did you get it so quickly?" he asked.

She glanced at him. "I purchased it ages ago when I first went into service."

Matteo frowned. "Then you didn't get it because of me? Because of what you thought I might do?"

His voice was a low rasp, but he looked at her expectantly until she answered.

"No."

"You were prepared to run away? Why? Was there someone else who was bothering you? One of the other servants or a local man?"

The concern in his voice seemed discordant and wrong after everything that had happened.

"No."

"Then why?" he asked softly.

"I promised my mother."

His brows drew together. She expelled a breath and decided to explain. He already knew her darkest secret. There wasn't anything else for her to hide. It might even make him understand how unprepared she was to deal with his problem.

"She made me promise on her deathbed that no matter what occurred, I would never use magic or reveal to anyone that I was even capable of it. Sometimes things happen around me, things I can't control. I have to be vigilant."

"And that's why you stopped your magic lessons? Because of your mother's passing?"

"No, that happened earlier. I had been studying the craft with my grandmother when my aunt Moira died. My mother demanded that all lessons stop. She forbade all talk of magic. I was heartbroken, but there was nothing I could do, not after my father took her side."

"How did your aunt die?"

Isobel wrapped her arms around herself. "I'm not sure, but I know she used her magic to hurt someone. The man she was supposed to marry. He'd decided to marry someone else because they had a larger dowry and she was heartbroken...and then angry. She decided to take revenge."

"Did she kill him?"

"I don't think so, but he was hurt—maimed. My aunt had exposed herself with that act. I'm not sure how she actually died, but when word of the scandal reached us, the village's attitude changed. The long years my grandmother had spent as healer in the community didn't matter. We were tainted. My mother publicly broke with my grandmother so she and I wouldn't be ostracized. The effort was only partially successful. Not everyone was cruel, but enough of them were. My father's position as a gentleman farmer helped shield us from the worst of it, but I still remember how they treated us."

She didn't mention the likelihood that her aunt had died after being hunted down by the man's relatives. It wasn't something she liked to dwell on. Enough time was spent on it in her nightmares.

"Did anyone try to hurt you?" he asked, returning her back to the here and now.

Her lips pursed. "A few times. Some of the village boys chased me and threw rocks, but it passed after my father spoke to their fathers."

Matteo was frowning, but his voice was soft. "Your father sounds like a good man."

The pang in her chest made it hard to breathe. "He was," she whispered.

"And your grandmother? Did you ever see her again?"

Isobel nodded. "I would sneak over to see her. But she wouldn't teach me any more magic. Grandmother Helen was heartbroken by my aunt's death, and she respected my mother and father's decision. I pleaded with her to change her mind, but she never did." She paused and turned to him. "Can I ask you something?"

"Anything," he said.

"How did this happen to you? Who did you cross?"

He scowled at the muddy road. "What do you mean?"

"Who cursed you?"

He stopped walking. "Isabella, no one did this to me."

She choked on air, coughing in surprise. "Then did you do this to yourself? Are...are you a student of the occult?"

"Of course not! I just woke up one day like this."

Her brows rose. "No one simply wakes up cursed! You must have done something to upset or hurt someone. Something terrible."

"I swear to you no one did this to me," Matteo said, gesturing with his hands in that Italian manner she'd learned to recognize in the past few weeks. "There was no reason. I've never hurt anyone—not before this. It's unimaginable."

His words rang with sincerity.

Isobel shook her head, passing a hand over her eyes. "I don't know how to say this more clearly. There is simply no way you weren't targeted for this—this punishment. The spell afflicting you is pernicious and intricate. Someone spent a lot of time and effort crafting this spell. It can't have been done randomly."

The expression on Matteo's face was enough to stop her speech. He looked devastated.

"But I haven't *done* anything. Nothing that would warrant this. My life has been very structured, almost boring at times, which is why I enjoyed traveling." He stopped walking. "Is it possible I triggered a curse during my last voyage?"

"Not as likely. Not if you'd been home for weeks before it started."

He hung his head. "So you think it was someone from Santa Fiora?"

Isobel shrugged. "Do you suspect anyone?"

"No. I've tried to be a gentleman and a good son. I can't imagine that anyone bears this sort of ill will towards me."

"What about a scorned lover or someone jealous of you?"

He ran a hand through his neat hair, mussing it thoroughly. "I can't speak towards jealousy. I'm privileged and possess a fortune, but so do many other men. That's no reason to do this to me. As for former lovers, no."

Isobel raised a skeptical brow. Matteo was a grown man, one who exuded sexual appeal like a fine cologne. She didn't believe for a second that he'd had no lovers and said so.

Matteo turned red. "I didn't mean I hadn't had any, just that they would have no reason to do this. My last liaison was with...well, never mind. Someone who wouldn't be capable of this."

Frustrated, she abruptly turned around and started walking back to the inn. Matteo and his servant had to run to keep up with her.

When Matteo reached her side, she rounded on him. "If you're not going to be completely honest, there is nothing I can do for you!"

He looked embarrassed. "All right! My last lover was in Italy, what you would call a courtesan. Our relationship, such as it was, ran its course and she moved on to another protector. She was a woman of the world and was not very upset, not overmuch anyway. Not after she received my generous parting gift."

She slowed her steps. "What about other relationships? Jealous rivals or husbands?"

He scowled. "I don't sleep with married women. Well, not anymore."

She gave him a pointed glance and he sighed.

"When I was very young, maybe twenty or so, I did have a brief association with a married woman. But I soon learned that I was not her only lover, and I seriously doubt her husband knew about us. And if he did, I doubt he would have cared. He was conducting his own affairs. But, I didn't like that feeling of..."

"Cuckolding another man?" she supplied.

Matteo wrinkled his nose. "If you must, then yes. I steer clear of married women now. In any case, that was years ago." He fidgeted with this coat buttons and was quiet for a minute. "Could this curse have come from an object, something I touched that was meant for someone else?"

Thinking he meant his father, Isobel had to concede the likelihood. "It is possible, but I have to believe whoever did this knew what they were doing. If someone else was their target, then I think they would have tried again."

"Not necessarily," he protested. "We left home a few weeks after. Maybe they didn't get the chance."

She mulled that over. It was possible he was correct, but her instinct niggled at her. She wanted to disagree, but had no reason to keep arguing as they made their way back to the inn.

When they entered the taproom, Isobel nearly lost her hard-won composure. The *Conte* had arrived.

CHAPTER 12

*S*he was back in the private parlor, sitting as far from the count as she possibly could. They were alone. Sir Clarence had been left behind in Ford, a detail for which she was grateful. Isobel didn't think she could look at her former employer without screaming the place down. Or trying to claw his eyes out.

Matteo had gone to make arrangements with the innkeeper. They were renting the entire upper story. If other guests arrived seeking lodging for the night, they would have to look elsewhere. Even the empty rooms were rented to the *Conte*. Whatever the man had planned, he didn't want any witnesses.

Isobel sat ramrod straight. She wouldn't look at Aldo, but she could feel his eyes on her, weighing and assessing. Soon her anger overcame her fear.

She despised this man and his power over her. The fact that women in her position were so vulnerable to him and his like filled her with an acid hate.

Finally, he spoke. "You're what I came to England to find, you know. A witch powerful enough to lift the curse from my son."

She met his eyes. They were so similar to Matteo's, a rich dark brown. But his son—when he was himself—had such warmth in his. On the *Conte* they were cold, not completely lifeless, but close.

More like Matteo's other self.

She responded with a question of her own. One she knew he wouldn't like. "He's like this because of you, isn't he? Because of something you did?"

She didn't bother to use his title. Anyone who tried to kill her could be spoken to familiarly and without civility.

Aldo's face hardened. "Is he all right now?" he asked, making an effort to keep his voice polite.

He failed completely. Isobel knew he didn't care for her. He thought her beneath him. The *Conte* only respected his peers and probably very few of them at that. To have to speak to a governess, to depend on one for his son's life, must have been difficult for him. He probably considered it an insult to his person.

"I already told Matteo no. He's still afflicted. And I don't know how to help him. Not without knowing how and why he was cursed."

She wasn't about to admit that she didn't have the knowledge or the skill to cure his son. It had been on the tip of her tongue to tell him to find someone else, but she didn't want to give him any ideas. The *Conte* didn't value her life; she already knew that. Staying alive might mean making promises she couldn't keep.

Aldo glared down his nose at her. It was bigger than Matteo's, broader. There were other differences too. His son probably had more of his mother in him than the man would have wished.

"I don't know how this was done. I never even believed such a thing was possible until I saw Matteo change before my very eyes."

"How, exactly?"

The *Conte* sighed, his eyes growing distant. "He was sick for a few days. I was very concerned. We consulted a physician, but he deteriorated so quickly. The doctor told me to prepare for the worst, but I couldn't accept that. Some visitors had come to call. We were supposed to be hosting a house party that weekend. Instead, we turned them away, those that lived nearby. A few stayed."

Isobel nodded.

Aldo looked down, his face older than it had been a moment before. "Matteo had stopped answering questions or responding when touched. He was so cold. I thought I was losing my only child. I watched over him from a chair next to him. But I fell asleep. When I woke, he was gone."

"And then what happened?" she prompted when he stayed silent.

"I went looking for him. Instead, I encountered a maid running out of the study. One of my friends who lived too far to travel home was spending the night. Apparently, our guest had been having some fun with the girl in one of the parlors. When I went inside, this man was dead and Matteo was just sitting there staring blankly at the wall."

Isobel made an effort to smooth her features. "He was raping her, wasn't he?"

Surprised, the *Conte* looked up. "No, Matteo has never forced any of them."

This time she did frown. "I wasn't talking about *him*. I meant your *friend*. The one who was with the maid."

The *Conte* scowled at her. "She wasn't even pretty. I doubt he had to force her. And she was just a servant. What does it signify? What matters was Matteo. He'd killed someone—a peer."

She had to look down at the table to hide the cold rage that no doubt filled her eyes. Even cursed, Matteo had more regard for the poor maid than his father. Isobel didn't have any particular hatred of the aristocracy, but she did hate men like the count—men so filled with arrogance and disdain for those beneath them that they thought nothing of hurting the weak or turning a blind eye when others did.

The fact that it hadn't even occurred to him to be angry at his friend for having 'fun' under the same roof as his supposedly dying son—well, that was beyond the pale.

Closing her eyes and breathing deeply, she focused on burying her feelings. They would do her no good now.

"You said Matteo never...forced himself on his victims," she said, her throat tight.

"On the women? No, of course not."

Liar.

"Then why did you take *only* women? Maids and others from the lower classes. You could have just as easily taken men. Criminals—men the world would be better off without," she said, glaring at him.

The *Conte* gave her a cold look, examining her from head to toe before leaning back in his chair. "Sometimes we did. It wasn't always possible. Are you going to help my son, or do I need to find another witch?"

Anger bubbled up, getting the better of her tongue. "If you can, I would advise you to do so," she said between gritted teeth. "I can't do anything for him."

"Can't or won't?" The menace in the Conte's voice was clear, but Isobel refused to be cowed.

"You haven't told me anything that would be useful in finding a cure. No information on how or why he was cursed."

"Because I don't know!" he yelled.

Isobel flinched in spite of herself before she took a deep breath. "Then tell me what you do know."

His hands opened and closed. "What else is there?"

Isobel gripped the table. "How does he kill? You said he doesn't rape. You don't give him a weapon. Does he simply strangle the women?"

The *Conte* shook his head. "No. He barely touches them. They just die."

Taken aback, Isobel's mouth fell open. "How exactly?"

He rolled his eyes. "When the malady returned, I found what my son needed and did as I did with you," he said, choosing his words carefully. "It was the only thing that brought him back. But only for a short time—anywhere from a few days to a week. It used to be longer at the beginning. My servants alerted me to the strangeness of the bodies. They appeared pristine, completely untouched. So we watched a few times from a window or other vantage point."

Isobel shuddered slightly. The thought of the *Conte* and his men observing Matteo and his victims like an experiment, watching a predator with his prey, sickened her. But the *Conte* didn't care what she thought. He simply continued.

"After a certain point, you have to stay away from him. He goes very still and cold. Then the next person he touches dies. Man or woman, it doesn't matter. All he has to do is touch them. He puts his hands on them, and they convulse and fall down dead. That's all."

That's all.

Isobel had never heard of anything like this. And if he didn't rape any of his victims, what had he been about to do to her? He'd gone still and been icy cold, just as the *Conte* described, and he'd touched her. A lot, she thought pushing away her troubled memories of that night.

But she hadn't died.

"It's gotten more difficult," the *Conte* continued, snapping her back to attention. "The space between his bad spells is growing shorter."

"And so Matteo needs more victims," she said softly.

"It's not him doing the killing. It's the thing inside him," he said in a hard voice.

That much might be true. But it didn't explain Matteo's reaction that night. *Not her!* his voice echoed in her mind. She stifled the urge to cover her ears in an effort to drown out the memory.

The count's mouth firmed. "Your night with him is the only one when he's returned to himself without a death. So you will stay with him, day and night. If you want to go free, it will be *after* you have found a cure. In the meantime, do everything you can to make him happy. My son has been burdened by this long enough. He obviously wants you, so you're going to be his solace. I won't have him begging me to end his life—not again! I don't care what you have to do, but you will make him want to live."

He stopped then and rose to bang on the door. The smaller older servant, the one he called Nino, came in.

"Take her to my son," he ordered.

She didn't fight. This was not the time. Nino held her securely by the arm and guided her to the stairs.

"I'm very sorry, *signorina*," he whispered in English as they climbed.

Isobel gave him a sideways glance. Though small in stature, the man had once been handsome. But now he looked wasted and a bit tired, his face grey with deep grooves etched around his mouth. And he did appear genuinely contrite.

"Can you help me?" she asked quietly.

How exactly, she didn't know. It wasn't likely the count would let her go if his servant asked. But perhaps the man could convince Matteo.

Nino shrugged uncomfortably before looking around. "You should know...Ottavio always falls asleep during his watch. The second watch."

Suppressing a sigh, Isobel looked away. What good would that do her if Matteo was in the same room with her? Sighing, she hung her head. It was good to know Nino had some semblance of a conscience, but he wouldn't take any decisive steps to aid her.

She would have to help herself.

CHAPTER 13

*M*atteo woke up with a start when Isobel was shoved past the door of his chamber.

It was warm inside, the peat fire still burning cheerfully in the hearth. The strangely satisfying smoked earth smell had lulled him to sleep. He had dozed off in his shirtsleeves on the bed, but when she came inside he rose and they stared at each other.

She stood there, her back against the door, trying so hard to look brave and composed when it was obvious she was terrified. He didn't blame her. She had no way of knowing when he would succumb to another bad spell.

"I'm sorry. I should have waited for you," he said gesturing to a tray of food on a small table, a cold repast of game pie and vegetables he'd ordered in the hopes it would stay appetizing long enough for Isobel to finish her conference with his father.

Matteo had eaten his share distractedly earlier, and he regretted that now. He should have waited for her. As she looked at the tray, her stomach rumbled loudly and he smiled. She frowned. He stepped to the table to pour her a glass of watered-down wine before moving away, guessing she wouldn't want to come near him.

He sat on the bed, but her tension only increased.

And you know why, he thought, glancing down at the bed.

"I'll sleep on the floor," he said. "You don't have to worry about that. The last thing I want to do is hurt you."

"Then why can't I have my own room?"

He looked away, his hands opening and closing reflexively. "I'm sorry. I know you would be more comfortable in your own chamber, but my father feels it's safest if I'm with you. For all concerned. I didn't exactly have a say..."

It was the truth, but not the whole truth. Being close to her, even for a little while, was the only thing he had to look forward to in the difficult days to come.

Isobel wrapped her arms around her waist before walking to the table. She started to eat mechanically, eyes forward and distant. He sat in the corner, pretending to read a book while she finished. When she was done, he presented her with a package.

"I sent out for this. I wasn't sure you would have one with you," he said, opening the brown wrapping and pushing it toward her. "That dress can't be comfortable to sleep in," he added, nodding at the thick skirts of her widow's garb.

The gift was a nightgown, short-sleeved but modest with a high neckline, made of thick warm flannel.

"I also requested an extra blanket, so you can keep all the bedding to yourself," he said as Isobel fingered the fine cloth of the nightgown.

"I had a nightgown in my bag. It was on the carriage."

He nodded. "I'm sorry we misplaced your belongings. I have already sent word that it should be returned, and promised a sizable reward. It's possible it is already waiting downstairs. Would you like me to check with the innkeeper?"

Looking away again, she sat on the bed. "It can wait until tomorrow. This one will be warmer in any case."

"All right then. I'll wait outside while you change," he said, slipping out of the door and into the cold hallway to wait.

A door on his right opened, and Ottavio peered out at him with a frown. Matteo glared back at him.

Apparently, his father had ordered his minder to stay vigilant, despite having found Isobel. He stood in the hallway for a few more minutes before turning to tap on the door to let her know he was coming back inside.

~

ISOBEL UNDRESSED AS QUICKLY as she could. Fortunately, she'd had the foresight to buy stays and a dress with fastenings in the front, but the dress had many buttons.

She had just thrown the flannel nightgown on and was hastily climbing into the bed when there was a tap at the door and Matteo came back inside.

Embarrassed, she pulled the covers up to her chin, but the expression of dawning horror on his face stopped her.

"Your arms!" he rasped.

Isobel looked down at them, confused.

"What's wrong?" she asked stupidly, belatedly realizing the bruises on her arms were visible in the short-sleeved gown.

They were a dark black and blue, and quite startling against the pale cream of her skin.

"Did I do that? I did—didn't I?" Matteo's confusion was palpable. He was shaking his head. "I don't understand."

She stared at him, uncertain what to say. Eventually she took pity on him. "What don't you understand?"

"I don't do that!" he said, horrified. "I've never done that. I don't hurt them. They just die."

Isobel narrowed her eyes at him. "Your father said that too. That all you have to do is touch a victim, and they fall down dead."

He nodded emphatically. "That's what happens."

She cocked her head at him. "How can you be sure? You've already said you don't remember the events during...one of your spells."

Matteo collapsed in the chair and scrubbed his hands over his face harshly. "I told you. I've seen them after, once my memory clears. There wasn't a mark on them," he whispered.

"And were they dressed?"

His face turned fiery red. "*Yes*, they were. Although at first they were brought in their nightclothes or in a state of undress. My father assumed I would want them that way. But it wasn't about that. Once he realized the truth, he never bothered again." His voice sounded like sandpaper.

She pursed her lips and nodded, stifling the rush of anger she felt for those helpless men and women to focus on what he'd said. The details were consistent with the count's story. And while she believed his father would have lied to her, she didn't think Matteo would. He already believed the worst of himself.

"What you describe. The way things happen—it wasn't the same for me."

"I hurt you."

She nodded again.

"Badly?"

Gripping the covers tightly, she considered her answer carefully. "You hurt me some, but that was not your goal. You, or rather the thing inside you, wanted something else."

He didn't say anything for a long time. "You've always been different," he finally whispered, wiping at his face with a quick movement. Raising his head, his burning eyes met hers. "I'll make this right. I'll marry you."

Isobel's mouth dropped open. She cleared her tight throat. "There is no need. You didn't succeed in dishonoring me. I stopped you."

His face showed no reaction. "But I did try to...to...rape you."

Isobel stared down at her hands on the white coverlet. "Yes."

"*Why?*"

She stared at him in disbelief. How the bloody hell did he expect her to answer that?

Matteo flushed. "I meant, why would I do that with you and not any of the others? Does *it* know about you? About your magic?"

She frowned at him. "I don't see how, but even if it did, why would that make a difference?"

He threw up his hands. "Yet another thing I don't know. I'm

drowning in my own ignorance. Maybe your magic doesn't signify. Maybe it's just about you."

"What about me?"

"It knows I want you."

It was said simply, with no prevarication or embarrassment. Isobel could feel the heat in her cheeks as he stared at her, waiting for her reaction.

"And because *you* want me, *it* might want me as well?"

He shrugged helplessly. "Whatever the reason is, I'm sorry." He grabbed the spare blanket the maid had brought up earlier. "I'll let you sleep now," he said quietly, stretching out on the floor near the hearth.

It was far enough across the room that she could see him from the bed.

"All right," she whispered, wondering how in the world she was going to sleep with Matteo in the same room. Or any man for that matter.

As it turned out, her fears and concerns weren't enough. The stress and long flight from Ford had depleted her reserves, and not even her instinct for self-preservation was enough to keep her awake.

Her sleep was devoid of dreams.

CHAPTER 14

Sounds in the hall woke Isobel early. There was a minute of confusion before the events of the previous day came back to her. She sat up abruptly.

Matteo was still on the floor, one arm thrown over his face. She relaxed slightly, then hurried to get dressed before he woke up. Once she was decent, she crept up to the sleeping man.

Mouth pursed, she examined what she could see of his face. His color looked fine. Tentatively, she bent down and pressed her fingers to his hand. He was still warm, but he was stirring now, his breathing changing. Hastily she withdrew a few steps until the back of her legs struck the bed.

Matteo's arm fell, and he turned toward her. For a moment, he smiled at her as if he was confused and then his expression sobered.

"*Bongiorno*," he rasped in a hoarse morning voice, sitting up with stiff movements. "Have you called for breakfast?"

"No. Not yet," she said, sitting on the bed. "Are we staying here today?"

Matteo shook his head. "My father mentioned leaving this morning."

"To go where?"

"He mentioned going home to Santa Fiora."

Italy! Her stomach clenched. How would she get away from them in a foreign country? Her Italian was passable, but even if she managed to hang onto her widow's disguise she would never be able to blend in long enough to escape. And though she knew the essentials of the language, her accent was terrible.

The chances of getting a second opportunity are remote, she told herself. Not with the guards watching her as well as Matteo now. There would have to be another way.

I'm going to have to try and cure him.

But she couldn't do that alone. She needed her grandmother Helen's help.

"We can't. Not yet," she said. "I have to go home first, to Carrbridge, in the Highlands."

His brow creased. "Why?"

"My grandmother left me her books when she died. She knew my mother could never bring herself to destroy them, no matter what she said about magic. And my father was a very literary man who loved books. Grandmother knew they would be safe with him. They're hidden near our home—our former home, I mean."

His attention was caught. "And these are books on magic? On curses like mine?"

"Some deal with healing. They include recipes for tonics and poultices. But some of them do deal with spellcraft—I don't know how many. I also have no idea if they mention anything like what is happening to you."

Matteo stood and began to pace. "You said your education ended when you were a young girl."

"Just after I turned twelve."

"So you never had the opportunity to study these books?"

She shook her head. "For the most part they were too advanced for me. All that I learned, my grandmother taught me herself. But she was teaching me to be a scrupulous record keeper. Grandmother always said keeping careful records was one of the most important skills a witch could learn."

"And so she wrote her spells down," he said, his tone making it clear that it wasn't a question.

"She wrote everything down. As did her mother before her and her mother before that. There are a number of volumes."

Matteo stopped pacing, his eyes bright for the first time. "We must go get them. This is too important an opportunity to disregard. Are they really so many books?"

Isobel gave a tiny nod. "They fill two large trunks at least, although they might not all be related to magic. There would be books on the natural world, herbology, and animal husbandry as well."

He blinked. "Animal husbandry?"

"My grandmother raised swine."

"Swine?"

"Yes."

"For food?"

She flushed slightly. "Yes. And because she enjoyed their company."

His cough sounded suspiciously like a laugh. "I see," he said with a carefully composed expression.

"They're very intelligent." She sniffed.

"Pigs?"

"*Yes.*"

His features smoothed. "I've never noticed. I should pay more attention when visiting our livestock farm. I'm going to go find my father and tell him about the change in plans. I'm certain he'll want to leave without delay."

He hurried out of the room.

THE *CONTE* HAD RELUCTANTLY AGREED to a detour to the Highlands.

Isobel had never traveled in a carriage so fine, but its well-sprung wheels and deeply cushioned benches were no match for the muddy and pitted roads that stood between them and their destination. Especially when it began to rain again.

When the roads became nearly impassable as the weather deteriorated, the old man's temper went with it. Glaring at Isobel from his corner of the coach, he would shift restlessly and loudly. The volume of his sighs would increase if she was in any danger of nodding off.

Matteo did his best to keep his father's spirits up in the beginning but eventually gave up the effort. Instead, he would ask Isobel detailed questions about her life.

He didn't just want to know about her childhood, or the training she'd received at her grandmother's knee. He also wanted to know about her life after that, about her parents and time in service.

Despite her suspicion of him, she couldn't help but find his curiosity oddly sweet. Nevertheless, she kept her answers brief when in the presence of the count. Aldo didn't need to know anything about her. But it was harder to maintain her distance when she and Matteo were alone.

She could feel her own confusion around him. Matteo was so earnest and eager. It wasn't childlike in the least, but his manner struck her as that of an innocent, a youth with little experience of the world. Which was ridiculous. He was a wealthy lord in Italy, with all the privileges and freedoms money could buy. There was no way he hadn't experienced at least some of the same excesses of life that occupied the ton in London.

But if he had, he didn't seem touched by it.

Isobel could feel her determination to keep the young lord at bay waning every day. She tried to hold onto her resentment and distrust, but it was difficult when he was being so kind and solicitous.

At every stop, Matteo would do anything and everything to ensure her comfort. He made the coach stop in Edinburgh long enough to buy her a warmer cloak, despite the count's vociferous complaints. When they would change horses on the road, he would make sure she ate and drank her fill before they continued and would order hot bricks wrapped in flannel for her feet and hands before they departed.

The first few times he forgot to ask for additional bricks for his father, an oversight the *Conte* let him know displeased him in blistering Italian as soon as they left the coaching inn.

Isobel had tried to hand over her second brick to the man, but

Matteo grew agitated, claiming that she needed to be at her best when they arrived in Carrbridge to take possession of her library. His logic silenced the count's complaints, but he still glared and sulked openly. At the next inn, Aldo ordered his own bricks.

She was going mad cooped up in the carriage all day, but it was the nights that filled her with tension.

Every night, the coach would stop at the best inn available. They would eat a relatively silent meal and then she and Matteo would be shown upstairs to the same chamber.

Once inside the room, Matteo would give her privacy to change by turning his back if there was no screen available. Then he would make a pallet on the floor and stretch out. She knew he had to be sore and uncomfortable after being in the coach all day, but he never complained. He seemed content to talk with her from his prone position on the floor, his hands behind his head.

Outside of the count's oppressive company, Isobel answered more of Matteo's questions in greater detail and in turn he would tell her stories, mostly about his childhood—especially the months spent on the shores of the Lago di Bolsena at one of their country estates.

He also described the famous sights of his homeland, interweaving what he knew of their history to entertain her. Though she was often tired when she heard them, his anecdotes blended in her mind until the image of the Tuscan countryside solidified and became real—a place of heated beauty and a noble, if somewhat frenzied, history.

In time she grew bold enough to make some inquiries of her own. Envious of the freedom his sex and wealth afforded him she asked him about his travels. Pleased to have found a subject of interest to her, he spoke of the crumbling Colosseum in Rome and the ancient sites of Greece, as if he would show them to her someday.

And every night he would promise to do whatever he could to ensure her safety and future happiness until she almost started to believe him.

Though it was impossible to bar the two of them inside their chamber without suspicion, Nino and Ottavio were always nearby. If the adjoining room wasn't available, then they slept on the floor in the hallway. The *Conte* had made no effort to excuse such behavior to people he considered inferior, but Matteo always made it a point to chat with the innkeeper in his lyrically accented English.

He passed off the guards as a necessary circumstance due to a mysterious incident at a lower quality inn. The details of his story were purposely vague, but they would always sympathize, especially when he implied that *her* safety was the real issue—the safety of his bride.

Isobel was always given strange looks when Matteo introduced her as his wife. She knew he was just trying to protect her reputation, but her choice of disguise bothered the staff and other visitors. Her clothes were suited to deep mourning, and Matteo's excuse that it was on his mother's account didn't seem to convince everyone when he wasn't also in black.

Occasionally she heard whispers. Some gossiped about the oddities of the Italian people, while others questioned her and whether or not she might have remarried without observing the proper mourning period. No one had yet guessed that she wasn't married at all, at least not out loud. A few might have suspected, however, given the way the count's expression soured whenever Matteo introduced her as his bride.

Her strange surreal existence continued until they finally entered her home county. The sights became familiar despite the fact they were still several dozen miles from her home. Apprehension filled her as they stopped at a posting inn near Ellan Wood. Though the innkeepers and the locals who frequented the tavern wouldn't know her face, they would have been familiar with her father's name. And Matteo wasn't keeping her identity a secret.

Soon they would be in Carrbridge, surrounded by the people who had shunned her and the other women in her family. And day-by-day, the darkness inside of Matteo grew just a tiny bit more.

CHAPTER 15

*D*espite the dreadful weather, the majesty and sweeping vistas of the Highlands took Matteo's breath away. It was an unforgiving landscape, most unlike the warm and welcoming peaks and valleys of his home. But there was a rugged and imposing beauty to this place that spoke volumes about the character and fortitude of its inhabitants. It made a great deal of sense that this was Isobel's birthplace.

He had expected her to exhibit some growing excitement about seeing her home after such a long absence. Instead, she grew quiet and pale. Her hands were still on her lap, but she betrayed her tension with the way she gripped them together tightly.

Matteo felt guilty for a whole new reason. Isobel had probably never expected to see this place again. The dark and unpleasant memories of her and her grandmother's treatment at the hands of the more ignorant locals coupled with the loss of both her parents surely made this homecoming difficult, to say the least.

And there was another problem. Isobel was still known here. A maid at the last inn had recognized her. Apparently, his witch possessed the distinctive features and coloring of the women in her family.

It would not have been a problem if the locals believed Isobel was his wife as they should have, but their whispers indicated otherwise. They painted Isobel with a dark brush. In their eyes, she was already corrupt, a fallen woman with no virtue. He was her lover, a paramour literally enthralled by her sorceress' spell. It didn't help that the innkeepers avoided him, making it impossible for him to charm them into believing the story that she was his wife.

He made his decision on the way to the next inn, the one in the village where Isobel had grown up. She would have to marry him—here, before their very eyes. It was the only solution. The doubting Thomases of the villages would be satisfied that Isobel's reputation was intact if they were actually wed in Carrbridge.

If he didn't and the worst happened to him her reputation would be in tatters, even if she somehow escaped his father. She could never be a governess again, not if a future employer looked into her background. Even a whiff of scandal was enough to destroy her character, and the sphere of high society was smaller than anyone realized. Because of him, Isobel would be defenseless and without resources, unable to earn a living.

But if they were married, her status as his widow would protect her forever. Isobel would bear his name, and he could leave her all or part of his fortune—the piece that was independent of his father and the estate. The count would be forced to deal with her fairly.

Especially if she bears you a child.

His heart picked up and his body grew warm as he stole a sidelong glance at his witch. She was looking out the window on the other side of the carriage, the fine line of her cheek and neck silhouetted against the light of afternoon. The deep longing he had been trying to bury surfaced, nearly overwhelming him.

He would speak to her tonight.

THE STREAK of darkness in Matteo's aura had become more pronounced. It wasn't as dense as when she'd met him in the Montgomery home, but it was there, no longer hiding from her mind's eye.

The corruption was slowly building inside him. To make matters worse, she was home.

The village of Carrbridge hadn't changed much in the years since she'd left. The bakery had an addition built, and the Lawsons had knocked down one of the shacks they called tenant cottages and finally built a new one. Other than that, the place was startling in its sameness.

She doubted her former neighbor's attitude to her and her family had changed much, either. If she'd been alone, her reception would be icy, to say the least. But with an Italian count and his son in tow, well, there was no saying how the village would react.

Distracted by her memories, she dragged herself from the carriage with little enthusiasm. She didn't bother with her veil—there was no hiding from the past. Not here.

Once inside the inn, she could feel dozens of eyes on her. Exhausted and consumed with morbid thoughts she kept her eyes on Matteo's back as he introduced himself and asked for rooms.

"One for myself and one for my fiancée, Isobel," he finished.

"Fiancee?" the innkeeper asked, his wide eyes swinging to hers.

Isobel froze, her face impassive as Matteo continued. "Yes, my lovely betrothed is from these parts. We came here to be married. We meant to come in finer weather, but our plans were delayed by the unfortunate death of my mother," he said, gesturing to Isobel's black gown. "But the time of mourning is over, and I didn't want to wait a minute longer to make this beautiful creature my bride. I trust the old magistrate Isobel mentioned is still alive? I'd like him to perform our wedding, just as soon as we find the perfect location..."

Her head filled with a formless buzzing as Matteo enthusiastically detailed their wedding plans. The innkeeper, whom she vaguely remembered as being friendly with her father, gave her a genuine smile and bent to kiss her hand in congratulations. Both Matteo and his father frowned upon the familiar gesture, but they were soon distracted by the flow of regulars that rose to offer them their felicitations.

Most of the people she recognized, although the majority looked like they had aged more than the four years she'd been absent. Almost all of them restricted their warm greetings to her fake fiancé. At best she got a distant nod. No one but the old innkeeper—Tom?—tried to touch her, which was probably for the best considering the flare up she'd seen in Matteo's aura when his hands had made contact with hers.

When the noise and crowd became too much, Matteo led her to the private parlor the ladies of the village used for their Bible study, while the count went upstairs to inspect the available rooms.

Matteo shut the door behind them and led her to a weathered chaise lounge. She didn't realize that she was trembling until he took both her hands in his.

"My lord, how could you say that? Now they'll be expecting a wedding!" she hissed, her eyes wide.

He knelt down in front of her. "Isabella, it's the only way. We have to get married."

She withdrew her hands and shook her head violently. "You could have said we were already wed, like before."

"No," he said quietly. "That's not possible...and it's my fault. I should have realized."

"Realized what?" she asked, slightly dizzy with confusion and anger.

"You're simply too recognizable here. And what you said about the locals—how they feel about your family—still holds true. The staff at the last inn didn't even let me explain that we were man and wife. Unfortunately, it's all too clear that the people who know and distrust your family still want to believe the worst of you. They won't accept that you're my wife unless they see us married with their own eyes. And..." He trailed off and looked down.

"And what?"

He reached for her again before stopping short. His head drew back. "I will not pretend that any of this is fair. I have already asked so much from you. But I've been thinking about how this is going to end. I know the chances of you finding a cure for me are very slim. And when this is over, when I'm gone, you are going to have a problem. Two problems really. Your reputation, and my father."

She was starting to have some idea of what he was thinking, but the reality of what he was proposing was simply too much take in.

"Both of those problems would be solved by our union," he continued. "It would not do for a man in my father's position to be seen mistreating his daughter-in-law. And you would have access to my fortune and the protection of my name."

The way he was avoiding her eyes told her this wasn't just about what he was offering—it was also about what he wanted.

"But this marriage will be a *real* marriage, won't it?"

Matteo finally met her eyes, the emotion in them so intense she flinched. "Isabella," he rasped, "in all likelihood, I have very little time left. If you fail, I will end this...this existence myself. I can't hurt another innocent. I refuse to be the devil's instrument."

He fisted his hands and looked away "However..." she prompted.

With a heavy exhalation, he sat next to her. "However, if I can spend the rest of my days, be it weeks or months, as your husband then I will die in peace, having gleaned what little happiness I could from this damned life. I know it would be next to impossible for you to forgive me for what happened that night. I saw the marks I made and I know how you suffered. But if there's anyone who could understand *that* was not the real me, it's you."

Isobel squeezed her eyes shut and gripped the cushion of the chaise lounge to steady herself. It felt like the world was spinning. A part of her wanted to absolve him, to ease the torment in his eyes, but she wasn't ready to do that yet.

"And...maybe there would be a child," he said, taking her breath away. "A tiny bit of myself and of you that would get to start all over again and live this life better than I did. With you as its mother, there's no possibility he or she wouldn't be remarkable. You would raise our child with your purpose and strength—"

"Stop! Stop..." she said finally, holding up her hands. Dropping her head, she exhaled.

The air moved as he shifted closer to her. "I swear I'm going to spend all of my time loving and cherishing you for as long I can—anything to make sure you don't regret marrying me, even for a short while. Whatever I can do for you, I will do." He paused. "Isabella, *mi amore*, there isn't another choice."

His voice sounded like it was coming from very far away.

Dizzily, she nodded. "I know," she whispered.

CHAPTER 16

$\mathcal{W}$hen Matteo revealed that his plans to marry Isobel were genuine, his father's thunderous expression could have stripped paint from the walls.

"Don't even think it," Aldo glowered at him when he got him alone in his room to explain.

Matteo glared back. He'd given way to his father on a lot of things, but this wasn't going to be one of them.

"You *will* support me in this," he said in a tone hard enough to make his father sit up in attention. "Isobel is my only chance for recovery, and I won't have her reputation destroyed because she was forced to help me."

He sat back in the uncomfortable extra chair the inn had moved into his father's room so he would have a place to converse in private.

The count opened his mouth to argue with him again, but Matteo cut him off. "And there is a chance the closest I'll come to recovery is extending my time long enough to sire an heir."

His father leaned back and considered his words before dismissing them with a wave of his hand. "You don't have to marry the witch. We'll take her and this library back to Santa Fiora. Bed her if you must, but you can marry one of the young ladies from home. Donneto's girl, perhaps."

Neck rigid, Matteo shook his head resolutely.

The count leaned forward. "You were meant for better things and you will not disgrace your family now. She is beneath you," he hissed.

The censure in his father's voice would have been enough to make him retreat once, but that was before he'd been damned. He no longer had anything to lose.

"There could be no finer union for me than one with Isobel. She is gently bred with a fine education, or else Clarence would never have hired her. And while she does not possess a fortune, she does have something more important."

"And what might that be?" his father asked sarcastically.

"Power," he said honestly, playing his strongest card. "Even now, without her books and the knowledge in them, she has it. And if her family history holds true, then our child would have it."

His father's face softened, his attention finally caught.

"I can imagine it now," Matteo said enthusiastically. "Our son would know the things Isobel does—the ability to see evil in those around them. And he would be *ready*."

The implication was clear. Isobel's child would grow up with the ability to defend him or herself against the forces of darkness, the same thing they'd found themselves completely unprepared for.

Matteo's shoulders dropped, and he looked down at his hands. "Isobel is not just *my* salvation," he whispered. "She's *our* salvation. For all the Garibaldis."

It was the simple truth, one even his father could see.

Aldo sighed loudly. "Very well. I will support the marriage."

MATTEO WAITED until well after midnight before sneaking into Isobel's room. His father had consented to their marriage, and to the need to keep up appearances. He and Isobel could not share a chamber before the wedding, but the count feared Matteo's deterioration too much to allow him to sleep without her.

He crept in as quietly as he could. But it wasn't quietly enough. Isobel looked up from the window, startled, her eyes wide in the moonlight that filled the room. She was still dressed, with her bag at her side. One of her legs was slung over the windowsill.

He was too numb to feel the disappointment or the pain. He'd asked for too much.

She had every right to run away from him. Here in Carrbridge, she might even have a chance of permanently escaping his father. It was true the locals didn't favor her, but maybe they would take her side if she revealed the truth about him and what he had done.

At the very least, she knew this place. No doubt every path and hidden corner was as familiar as the back of her hand. She'd been prepared in Ford, had admitted to learning the paths in the woods and possible bolt-holes during her days off when he'd questioned her late one night. That would have been a lesson learned early.

"It's all right," he whispered when she continued to stay there, frozen on the sill. "Go now."

Across the room, Isobel hung her head and her shoulders shook as if with a silent sob. Before he knew it he was there, his arms around her. He pulled her back inside and she burrowed into his chest, her arms squeezing him tight.

Her tears wet his shirt, but she made no noise. Matteo held onto her, slowly warmed by her breath filtering through the cloth of his shirt until she eventually pulled away.

Isobel turned back to the window and for a moment he thought she was going to go through it. He wouldn't stop her. Instead, she closed the pane, wiping her eyes on her sleeve as she faced him once more.

"The magistrate's name is Finchley," she said hoarsely. "And he's not old. He was new to his post when I left and from what I remember is a rather vain man. He'll probably be annoyed with me when he hears you said that. And he *will* hear of it. No doubt every word you said to the innkeeper has already spread over the entire village."

"What?" he asked, confused.

It was hard to follow what she was saying because she'd begun to undress. She had opened the lacings of her gown and was pulling it down to reveal a snowy white chemise. Her eyes avoided his as she pulled off her boots and climbed into bed.

"Not to mention that it's usually the minister that marries people in these parts," she added, pulling the covers up to her chin.

He stared at her for a long moment, relief flooding his chest. "Unless he's Catholic, my father won't want him marrying us."

Isobel shrugged. "Then the magistrate will have to do. Come to bed, Matteo," she whispered gesturing to the empty space next to her with a tiny movement of her hand. "It's going to be a long day tomorrow."

The joy he felt was making him stupid and slow. Mechanically, he took off his waistcoat and boots. He kept his breeches on and would sleep in his shirtsleeves. Shifting the bedclothes, he slipped underneath the coverlet next to Isobel, being careful not to touch her...until she reached out and took his hand, testing the top of it tentatively before pressing her palm to his.

Closing his eyes, he relaxed. His witch wasn't going to leave him.

CHAPTER 17

*I*sobel fingered the fine blue cloth of her new gown as the droning voice of the magistrate carried to her as if from a great distance.

Although the countrified style of the dress wouldn't have satisfied the snobs in a London ballroom, she found it lovely—even though it did not fit quite right. It was an inch too long, and the bust was a little tight and fell too low. Although, judging from Matteo's expression when he saw her in it, that last detail didn't bother him too much.

He had presented her with the gown early that morning with an apology. The dress was the best that could be gotten on short notice. Matteo had told the local seamstress that one of her trunks had been lost on the road, her wedding trousseau with it. Even if he didn't think the dress fashionable enough, Isobel had simply been grateful she wouldn't be married in black.

Speaking of which.

The droning had ceased. Raising her chin, she found the magistrate looking at her expectantly. On her left, Matteo shifted and gave her an encouraging nod. Parting her lips she murmured something, feeling wool-headed and slightly numb.

She didn't know what words actually came out of her mouth, but they must have been the right ones because Matteo relaxed and beamed at her. The rest of the service blurred. The long-winded sermon finally wound down, papers were signed, and congratulations flew.

The ceremony was followed by tea with the magistrate and various locals who had conveniently come to call that morning. The count was included in that number.

Isobel could have been knocked over with a feather. Aldo was doing a credible job of appearing pleased with the marriage. The obvious wealth betrayed by his wardrobe and his entertaining, though condescending, conversation was enough to awe the small villages' inhabitants.

Being the cynosure of so many curious eyes was exhausting. She made polite, if stilted, conversation with the locals, wishing for nothing more than for all of them to disappear. Fortunately, both the *Conte* and Matteo were too focused on getting to her grandmother's books to suffer their company for long.

They excused themselves and, after making sure they were not followed, headed into the hills to the east. Isobel led them to the ruins of an old fortification where they were joined by the count's servants.

The ruins were so old they didn't have a name. The history of the place, who had lived here and what they did, were details lost to time. The site wasn't as well known as the bridge for which the town was named. In truth, few people still visited the place, mainly because there was little left above ground.

Matteo had been impressed with the ruins, but she couldn't help but feel that his enthusiasm was a bit exaggerated. The few scattered stones and foundation remnants couldn't possibly compare with the ancient sights of Rome or the artistic treasures of Florence and Venice.

Once they were sure there were no other visitors about, Isobel led them away from the ruins into the neighboring wood. There she located the hidden entrance to a long forgotten tunnel that led to the old dungeons and storage rooms underneath the keep. Her father had told her it was likely an escape route for the inhabitants, should the fortification have fallen under attack.

Picking her way carefully with the torches the servants Nino and Ottavio had brought, they walked deep into the ground. In a few steps the space opened up until the rough stone walls more closely resembled rooms and storage cubbies. Some parts had collapsed, the ground blocked by old masonry and stones.

"Is this place sound? Or will the ceiling fall down on our heads?" the *Conte* asked, giving the walls a dubious glance.

"It's been falling for hundreds of years," she said honestly. "As long as we're careful, we should be fine."

He shot her a frown before turning away.

Matteo walked forward. "Where do you think the trunks are?" he asked, glancing around him, his eyes bright and eager as he examined every fallen rock and pebble.

"Over here."

She led them to the back wall, where a sizable amount of the ceiling had collapsed and partially blocked the entrance to one of the storage spaces. She pointed to the pile of rubble. "They're under here."

Matteo examined the debris. Some of the pieces were quite large. "Very clever. How on earth did your grandmother move all of these heavy stones by herself?"

"She didn't," Isobel whispered, as Matteo gestured for Nino and Ottavio to help him start shifting the stones. "It was my father."

"Your father?" he asked, turning abruptly in her direction, a fistful of masonry falling out of his hand. "I thought you said he didn't approve of you studying magic."

Sitting on one of the larger fallen stones, she nodded. "It's true, but only after what happened to my aunt. I told you he was open-minded. He was also a scholar, one who would rather cut his own arm off than destroy a book." She nodded at the pile. "He brought the trunks in here, empty, and then filled them a few books at a time. Afterward, he showed me where they were, in case I was ever in a position to claim them. He did express a wish that I not do so unless I was living elsewhere. I was fourteen at the time."

Matteo nodded, but was too busy to ask any more questions. Between the three men, they quickly uncovered the top of the first trunk.

"This is much larger than I thought it would be," he said eventually. "We'll never be able to carry them out without being seen. I think we should go and fetch the carriage. There's a path leading to the ruins large enough for it, isn't there?"

Isobel nodded.

"Then we should be able to drive it close enough to carry them out of here one at a time."

"You're going to put these filthy things in my carriage?" the *Conte* asked, his scowl fierce.

Matteo rolled his eyes. "Since we don't have the second carriage for the luggage, yes."

The old man scowled. "Can't you go buy a farmer's cart?" he asked, exasperated.

"Not without announcing what were doing to the entire neighborhood."

Aldo stopped complaining, but he glared at Isobel as if he blamed her for the state of the trunks while Matteo gave a few quick instructions to the men in Italian. Then he turned to her and offered his arm.

"I will take you to the cottage and return with the coach."

"What cottage?"

"We rented one for the week, until the weather improves. The innkeeper told me about it, suggesting that newlyweds need privacy," he said with a sideways glance as he led her out of the tunnel. "My father will stay at the inn."

He didn't have to tell her that the 'servants' would stay with them.

"We're staying a week? I suppose that might be enough," she said absently. "But I've been thinking we shouldn't go far."

His brow drew down as they stepped out of the tunnel into the fresh air. "What do you mean? I thought you'd be eager to depart, to leave the past behind."

Though he wasn't wrong, Isobel had thought of an important reason to linger in the neighborhood. "A number of the healing spells and poultices in those books may require local herbs. There are some growing wild in these hills, though they'll be fewer of them now with the cold. Others might be going fallow in my grandmother's old garden. We need to gather as many of them as possible and their seeds. That might be important. There will be a few locals who keep their own stores. We should offer to buy as much as they're willing to spare. The plants in Italy would be different, unfamiliar. Some substitutions might work, but others may prove unpredictable."

"I hadn't considered that," he said softly. "If we managed to get seeds, we could grow them ourselves."

"*If* we managed to get seeds. And they might not grow in a different climate."

He laughed unexpectedly. "Isabella, everything grows in Italy."

She frowned. "Do you want to wager your life on that?"

Matteo sobered. "I'll give it more thought."

They walked in silence for several minutes. When they crested the hill, Isobel paused, looking at the familiar gabled farmhouse nestled in the rise of the hill opposite. Below it was a lovely little valley with its own stream. Sheep grazed in the green fields nearby.

Her chest compressed tightly. Soon the house was blurred, seen through a haze of tears.

A large arm wrapped around her shoulders. "What is this place?" Matteo whispered.

Isobel pulled her cloak more tightly closed.

"My home. Well...someone else's home now."

"Oh." He examined the distant buildings. "It's very picturesque. You must have loved growing up here."

"I did," she said slowly.

"Was it entailed? Did another male family member inherit?"

Taken aback, Isobel turned to him. "No, it wasn't entailed. We had to sell it to pay my father's debts. Debts we didn't even know about till after he died..."

The last was said with a bitterness she couldn't hide.

Matteo frowned. "Unfortunately, being a good businessman

doesn't always come with a fine education. My father has to hire business managers because he can't do percentages to save his own life."

"That's true for many peers," she said distantly, a coldness settling in the pit of her stomach. "But my father was a good businessman. Conservative and careful. He would never have risked our livelihood with a risky venture."

"I don't understand. What happened?"

Digging her fingernails into her palms, Isobel stared down at her childhood home. "My father had just died, a bad fall from his horse. Then a pair of his former associates came with a note for the house. They claimed he had mortgaged it to them to finance a new mining venture down south. The investment had failed and they were here for the house. But my father had never mentioned any such scheme. And he always discussed his investments with my mother. That news, coming so soon after his death, was too much for her. She took ill and passed away before we even had a chance to pack anything. Not that they would let us take much. They insisted on keeping the contents of the house to repay the debt."

"I'm so sorry," Matteo said tightly. "I can buy it back for you if you like."

"No!" Breath labored, she turned away and stalked off in the direction they'd been walking in.

"Isabella! What's wrong?"

She kept walking, but his long legs kept pace with her easily.

"I didn't mean to offend you. I just thought getting back your childhood home might be a good way of securing your legacy in case I don't survive," he murmured.

Her steps slowed, and she hung her head. "It's not that. Your offer is generous, but I will never live here again."

He caught up with her, a light of realization dawning on his face. "You think they lied. Your father's associates…"

"I know they did."

Matteo gave her another comforting hug, pressing her body to his more intimately than before. He waited until she relaxed in his embrace before letting go.

"Was there nothing you could do? No one to appeal to?"

"These men, Lindsey and McNab, were elders of the town. There was no one willing to take up our cause. And they were seen as selfless because they didn't add the proceeds of the sale to their personal fortunes. They donated everything to the church." She clutched his arm. "It was *never* about the money. It was about getting rid of the witches. These men had been among the first to denounce my grandmother Helen when news of Moira's death reached us. Many others followed suit, but it began with them."

The cold was gone. Blood rushed hot in her veins as her anger flared. At their feet the grass swayed and danced counter to the direction of the wind chilling them. But Matteo didn't seem to notice.

Her new husband leaned over her, a dark light in his eyes. "Isabella, I don't pretend to have any influence here, but my fortune is extensive. If you want to investigate these men's dealings, I can hire someone. We could turn their lives over with a fine-tooth comb and expose them. Any of their sins would come back to haunt them tenfold. I can make sure of it."

Inexplicably some of her own anger lost its heat in the face of his indignation. Isobel had never had a defender or a champion, not since her parents died.

Matteo fit the mental image of avenging knight all to well. But he had arrived on his white steed too late. The time for vengeance had passed.

"Unfortunately, there is no one to focus your scheme on. Both men were old when all this occurred. They've gone on to their great reward," she said sarcastically. "If you want to punish their co-conspirators, you'd have to target half the town."

His gaze caught hers, his eyes soft on her face. "I understand. But I'm still sorry."

What was left of her fury drained out of her, leaving her empty. "Me too."

He put a hand on the small of her back and they continued on their way.

CHAPTER 18

*I*sobel and her new husband arrived at their destination shortly afterward.

She had been apprehensive at the mention of another cottage. But this recently built two-story structure in no way resembled the tenant cottage on the Montgomery estate. It had four spacious rooms in addition to the kitchens and scullery. The house sat at the far end of the Donnelley farm, one presumably used by their visitors or estate manager during the growing season.

A few maids from the inn were bustling around the ground floor when they entered, finishing preparations Matteo had ordered earlier that day. They had left food in the kitchen, cleaned the house from top to bottom, and placed fresh linens on the bed.

The girls left almost as soon as Matteo and Isobel arrived, promising to deliver a message from Isobel to the Old Meg, the local midwife. There was a lot of winking over that, and she knew they assumed she was already with child. It certainly explained the hasty marriage.

"Why do you want to see the midwife?" Matteo asked once they had left.

She couldn't suppress a small smile at the confusion in his voice.

"Do you need someone to speak to before..."

Isobel flushed. "No, although I probably should ask her some things, now that you mention it. But Meg is one of the people who gathers and keeps local herbs in these parts. And she was friendly with my grandmother after the scandal, although not openly."

"Oh, I see." He nodded. "I should get back to the ruins, but before I do—about tonight. I'm...I already knew you were innocent in every way that counts..."

She raised a brow, "Yes, and...?"

Ahead of her, her large and muscular husband shuffled his feet like a youth.

"I had assumed, you see—a governess is very vulnerable. But it's obvious now that you can take care of yourself. However, you might have succumbed to loneliness. I wouldn't blame you if..."

Embarrassed, Isobel looked away. "I did not become lonely."

A touch on her cheek surprised her. He had kneeled in front of her, the blackness in his aura nowhere in sight.

"Everything will be well tonight," he said, unable to hide how pleased her admission had made him.

His hand was warm on her skin, and she in turn felt that warmth spread over her body. Blushing, she looked down as he pressed a quick and hard kiss to her lips before departing.

ISOBEL WAS PACING up and down the length of the cottage's small bedroom. It was five paces from end to end, which she traversed over and over as she waited.

She'd been able to bathe and brush out her hair before her husband joined her, sweaty and dirty from securing the library. He was washing in the kitchen, about to join her momentarily. After lighting a candle, she forced herself to stop her vigil and climb into the bed, pulling the bedclothes up to her waist.

There is nothing to fear, she told herself. Isobel had spent many nights on the road with Matteo and had been perfectly safe. There were no signs of him succumbing to the curse as before. He hadn't fallen ill and his body had kept its natural warmth, or at least it had on the few occasions she'd touched him in the last few days. For tonight, she would think of the man as her husband—nothing more.

And really, isn't that more than enough?

There were three large trunks downstairs, not two. That had been a bit of a surprise. She'd had no idea her grandmother's library was so extensive. Matteo had told her they would be hiring a second carriage to take everything away at the end of the week.

She'd been hoping they wouldn't be traveling farther than Edinburgh, but the compromise Matteo reached with Aldo had been London. They would go to town for the remainder of the little Season. The situation wasn't ideal, but the *Conte* had been adamant. Edinburgh wasn't good enough. If he couldn't go home to Italy, he would enjoy himself in London, where he had many friends.

The plan was to rent a house outside of town, one with a conservatory she could use to grow things. They would also hire an agent here in Scotland to collect herbs and powders from local apothecaries up and down the countryside. If necessary, they would engage men to scour the hills themselves, buying the things she needed.

Meg had also stopped by, her friendly smile missing a few more teeth than when Isobel had seen her last. The midwife had happily promised a healthy portion of her stock of the local herbs, for a nominal price. She assumed Isobel had decided to take up her grandmother's mantle as a healer, and she let her believe that. In a real way, it was the truth.

Isobel had also arranged for Meg or her daughter to send her whatever else she might need by post, with the promise of paying her handsomely for her trouble.

She was trying to distract herself by mentally reviewing the herbs that could still be found in the hills and woods during this time of the year and what she might need to preserve their potency.

All of these plans seemed unimportant when Matteo entered the room. He was wearing a clean pair of breeches and another one of those soft shirts, but he hadn't bothered to fasten it.

His hair was wet, and she wondered if he was cold. The fire was low in the hearth, and the room was a bit chilly. But she didn't feel cold. Quite the opposite.

Stop being a pea-goose, she lectured herself.

It was true her mother had never had a chance to speak to her about what would happen on this night, but Isobel had grown up on a farm. She had a fairly good idea of what was supposed to occur. And there was the fact she'd been in service and had been friendly with the staff at all of her positions. The lower classes were far less reserved when it came to discussing intimate matters than their social superiors...

Matteo grinned at her from across the room, a sensual and intensively private smile. Tensing, she squinted at him in the dim light, trying to assess how pronounced the darkness in his aura had become. There was barely a trace of it, and she relaxed—but only slightly.

"So everything is arranged with the midwife?" he asked.

She'd mentioned Meg's visit earlier when he'd come back to the cottage.

"Yes, between her and her daughter we'll have someone knowledgeable on all the local plants ready to supply us. It's not as good as being here ourselves, but I must admit I'd rather not spend any time here if I don't have to."

Matteo's face softened. "We won't be here long. I sent a messenger ahead asking for an agent to find us a house to let outside of London. Two houses actually."

"Two?"

"My father has elected to take a house in town, whereas I think we'll be better served by a larger one outside of town, one with a conservatory as we discussed."

That was the best news she'd heard in ages, and it must have showed on her face because her husband laughed.

She smiled and blushed. "I'm sorry."

"Don't be. I know how he can be. I'm simply used to it." He sat on the bed, taking his time to admire her in her modest nightclothes. "I had hoped you'd still be dressed, actually. I had looked forward to helping you undress, the first of my many duties as a husband."

Isobel's face flamed and she held her breath as he leaned in to kiss her forehead. He withdrew slightly and moved down, pressing another to her cheek and then her chin and neck.

When he finally reached her lips, she had parted them to suck in a much-needed breath. It made it easy for him to tease her mouth open with his tongue.

Startled, Isobel drew her head back sharply into the pillows to stare at him.

"Has no one kissed you before, *cara?*"

"Not like that," she said, wide-eyed.

He laughed and glanced down at his chest. She followed his gaze with a hot blush as he slowly removed his shirt and boots. He took her hand and placed it over his heart before moving it up to his lips.

Clasping it in turn, she tugged on his hand and he moved, crawling over her like a predatory cat.

His body came down over hers as he took her lips again. The kiss was more aggressive this time and hungrier. It robbed her of her senses as his body pressed into hers.

A flash of fear ran through her, the memory of that night intruding on this moment, but it passed as the warmth of Matteo's bare skin began to heat her own.

It was not him, she told herself firmly, before closing her eyes.

She wrapped her hands around his head and tried to mimic the movements of his mouth.

The sound he made was a cross between a moan and a gasp. It sent a little reverberation through her, a sensation of unexpected pleasure. Then he turned his head and blew out the candle next to her on the bedside table.

The faint glow of the fireplace gave only enough light to silhouette Matteo as he backed off of her. She heard the rustle of cloth as he removed his breeches. It was too dark for her to make out the details, but she had a brief glimpse of his erect manhood against the glow of the fire.

The sight was intimidating. Swallowing heavily she tensed as the covers were pulled back. Heat enveloped her, covering her in a blanket of hair-roughened skin and hard flesh.

His weight was temporary as Matteo moved down her body, tossing the blankets aside to run his hands up her legs, pushing the skirt of her nightgown up to her waist. She was expecting him to move back up again, so when he pressed his lips to the fragile skin of her sex she yelped and tried to push him away.

He parted the curls shielding her secrets and began to trace a path over her lips with the tip of his tongue.

"My lord, what are you doing?" she panted, confused.

There was no answer, only a heightening of sensation as he delved deeper. Startled, she pushed at his head harder until he took hold of one of her hands and kissed it.

"Relax *mi amore*," he murmured, pushing her down before resuming his intimate exploration.

Isobel tried to follow his direction but she couldn't. Instead, she lay back and stared at the ceiling, hands fisting, trying to grab something to hold on to. But the more he stroked and licked at her damp flesh, the weaker her grip became.

"Matteo!" she gasped as he pushed one of his fine patrician fingers inside of her.

He stroked and probed in concert with the movement of his mouth until he was moving in and out of her in a regular rhythm, his tongue running up and down over her most intimate skin.

She was breathing in a raged staccato pattern, her hips wriggling involuntarily when he slowly added a second finger, flexing and separating them slightly to open her wider. Flinching at the sudden discomfort, she let a little whimper escape before she could stop herself. He made a soothing sound and kissed her softly before sucking in the little nubbin of hooded flesh at the top of her sex.

It was like lightning had shot through her entire body. Her body arced as her body spasmed and clamped down on Matteo's fingers tightly. The hoarse cry that escaped her was involuntary and loud enough to embarrass her later. But Matteo murmured soft approving words in Italian she couldn't really understand as he crawled up her body and settled between her legs, his stone hard member pressing into her.

She couldn't help it—she tensed, the languorous pleasure dissipating like smoke. And he could feel it.

"It's all right, *mi amore*," he whispered, stroking the skin of her thigh.

She thought he was going to stop. Instead, he took hold of her hips and rolled until she was on top of him.

"What are you doing?" she asked, giving him a frown he couldn't possibly see with her back to the fire.

"This way will be more...comfortable for you this first time," he murmured, pushing her up until she was straddling him.

Slowly he lifted the hem of her nightgown up. The soft material brushed up her waist and against her breasts in a sensuous rush. Her sensitized skin tingled as she was freed from the restraint, the peaks of her breasts hardening in contact with the air.

Breathless now, Isobel tried to regain her scattered senses. But the hard male body underneath her shifted and her body quickened in a dizzying rush. Steadying herself she giggled suddenly. Matteo's brows rose.

"Er, I just realized why women are only allowed to ride side-saddle," she said as he gathered her closer.

He laughed, a deep rich sound that relaxed her more than anything else could have. His fingers stroked her damp flesh, teasing and thrilling her until his arousal began to press against the small opening of her entrance.

Her body resisted him with more determination than it should have, given what Matteo had just done to her. She couldn't see him, but he felt large, too large.

She cried out when her body finally gave way and the bulbous head of his shaft penetrated her body.

"Shh," he murmured, moving her legs to adjust her position once more.

He pulled her on top of him, the bare skin of his chest and stomach touching the smoother skin of hers. "Just wait a moment, and you'll grow accustomed to me."

Isobel gripped his arm. "I really don't think that's going to happen," she whispered.

"You will. The worst is over," he said, but his voice sounded strained.

He stroked her back, running his hands over her bottom before nudging his hips forward the tiniest bit. When she didn't complain, he worked himself in farther.

Isobel hissed as Matteo forged a path into her body. It burned slightly, but it wasn't truly painful anymore. Holding her tight to his chest, he moved his hips up and down until he filled her completely, his body flush against hers.

The sensation was different now. It was as if he was heating her from the inside out. There was still a little discomfort, but it was overwhelmed by the strange ticklish pleasure that accompanied his every movement. She moaned aloud, digging her hands into his sides as he moved faster and faster. The sensation built and built and it felt like she was coming to the peak as before, but it remained elusive.

"Isabella, are you close?" Matteo rasped, his breath short and fast.

"*Close?*" she asked in confusion.

"To another climax, like before..."

She didn't know what to say. The pleasure was there, but it wasn't as intense as when he'd used his mouth. He didn't wait for an answer, releasing her and urging her to sit up and straddle him again—guiding her until she was riding him in an irregular and slightly frenzied tempo.

"Oh!" she cried out as Matteo moved one hand to place where they were joined.

He rubbed and circled that mysterious little nubbin once more while his other hand pushed at her back, urging her down just enough to take her breast in his mouth. The dual stimulation was too much. Her channel fluttered and gripped Matteo inside her as she threw her head back and gasped.

His hands moved to her waist, holding her firmly against him as he rocked upward in repeated hard thrusts.

He ground into her almost painfully, but it didn't matter. The pain only heightened the sensation. It was as if a fire was burning behind her eyes, red tinted flames obscuring her vision as a wave of pleasure rolled over her. He cried out, the sound muffled and distant as she felt a spreading warmth inside her. Gripping her tightly he pumped his seed inside of her.

When her awareness returned, she had collapsed on Matteo's chest, which was moving up and down like a bellows. He was still inside her, hot and hard, but growing softer. His lips pressed against her forehead as his fingers traced patterns on her skin.

"Are you all right, *cara?*" he asked.

She nodded, but he didn't say anything else, as if he was waiting for her to speak more.

"That wasn't what I thought it was going to be like," she whispered eventually.

"What were you expecting?"

"Something less...wet."

Deep masculine laughter shook the bed. "I know you enjoyed it, even if it was more *untidy* than you expected," he said smugly before rolling slightly until she was lying on the mattress.

She ignored him as he chuckled and moved out of the bed, returning quickly. She was about to ask him what he had done when he knelt over her, pressing a cloth between her legs, cleaning her and then himself before climbing back into bed.

He slipped his hands around her while murmuring his appreciation and affection. They talked long into the night, eventually falling asleep side-by-side.

MEMORIES of the night before melded with images from her dream. Caught between those half-conscious illusions and the waking world, Isobel opened her body as large hands moved over her breasts and trailed down to her waist. Heat centered between her legs as she was carried by the rocking waves of a warm ocean.

Her eyes flew open as her husband began to push inside of her. He was behind her, the hand underneath her pulling her closer to him while the other moved between her legs, alternately stroking her sex or pulling her leg open a little wider to give him better access.

She gasped as she was filled, the position new and the pleasure intense. There was still a slight soreness from the night before, but her body was only too ready to accept him.

Time seemed to stop as Matteo wrapped his arms around her hips, his body pumping into hers again and again.

It didn't seem possible that the same feelings and thrills could occur in the morning light, but there it was, building and building until she gave herself over to it. Calling out his name, she shuddered in his arms, her body pressing back hard against his.

She was in a daze when he turned her over, covering her body as he pushed her into the mattress, confident now that she wouldn't tense and withdraw from him again.

Eyes closed, she felt him kiss her softened lips before he entered her from above, his broad manhood parting her sensitized flesh in a series of deeper and deeper thrusts...

Isobel opened her eyes to wrap her arms around him, but froze when she saw his face.

Matteo's skin was warm against hers, and his smile sweet. But his eyes were black.

CHAPTER 19

*I*sobel pulled book after book from the battered black trunk. She was surrounded by piles of them, her new blue dress stained from wrestling open the dirt-covered chests.

Her hands shook as she took the book and rapidly thumbed through it.

Calm down, she told herself sternly, taking deep and even breaths. But when she closed her eyes the memory of *its* face hovering over hers returned.

She didn't know what had happened. Matteo had been nothing like she remembered, or what the *Conte* had described. His skin had been warm to the touch, maybe a little cooler than normal, but nothing like the icy coldness of that terrible night. And he'd spoken to her, murmuring endearments the way the real Matteo did.

Oh, God.

Heart racing, she pressed the flat of her palms hard against her temples, physically trying to blot out the images flooding through her mind—and the physical memory of them. She could still feel his phantom touch all over, the way he had moved inside her and tasted the skin at her neck before he found his completion.

Its completion, she corrected.

And her body hadn't been able to tell the difference between the man and the monster. She'd been helpless to retreat, or stifle the response her body had been experiencing like a play that could have only one end.

No, she hadn't been able to stop it. Instead, she'd found ecstasy in a demon's arms. Then he'd collapsed against her, whispering her name tenderly before falling asleep almost immediately.

Why hadn't he killed her? Not just right now, but also the first time? Matteo had said she was different. At first she'd believed it was because her magic protected her somehow, but that wasn't the whole story.

By rights, she should be dead now. Contrary to all expectations, she was alive and well, allowed to move freely while he—*it*—slept upstairs. Matteo had slept all morning, the shade inside him dormant.

Somehow, she was exceptional to it. But he was different now too. Something she had done that night had changed him. Instead of a murderous automaton he was...well, she didn't know what he was.

She'd been watching, waiting for the evil to grow back and overwhelm him. Watching for the obvious had been a mistake. It had hidden from her, working itself in more deeply to him until she couldn't see where Matteo ended and the curse began.

What if, instead of temporarily alleviating him of his curse, she'd somehow bound him to it more tightly? If that was true, then this was all her fault. Her and her damnable ignorance. How could she possibly cure him now?

Isobel desperately wished she could speak to her grandmother. She would give anything for a few moments with her, or anyone who might be able to guide her out of this mess.

Running a hand through her disheveled hair, she tugged on it hard. Maybe the pain would give her focus. Putting the book down, she stood up to reach for another. And when that one didn't offer answers, she reached for another.

SIX DAYS LATER, Isobel was back in the carriage with the *Conte*, determinedly trying to ignore his continuous complaints. Her husband slumped against the wall, asleep. He'd been doing that a lot lately.

When he'd woken later that morning after their wedding night, she'd been expecting the worst. But Matteo had come down to join her in the library as if nothing had ever happened. His golden-brown eyes had been clear and his manner romantic and affectionate—the besotted groom on the first day of his honeymoon.

He'd immediately offered to help her sort through the books, taking up the task with energy and determination. Together, they organized a search of the countryside, gathering up what little herbs they could find with the help of Nino and, to a lesser extent, Ottavio.

There had been a bittersweet visit to her grandmother's home. She'd been surprised it was still standing. She'd been half expecting to find a burned out shell, but the locals must have feared the memory of her grandmother enough to leave the place alone. Matteo had inspected the contents inside, saving a decorative pitcher and a tray from the tea service for her. The precious plants and mosses from that garden and surrounding wood were cleaned and stored with the stock she'd received from Meg.

Throughout the week, Matteo behaved like the ideal husband, caring and considerate—and understanding when she told him resuming marital relations right away would be too uncomfortable. He patiently waited several days before asking again, though he hadn't been able to resist caressing or holding her.

Things had been so normal, she actually convinced herself that she'd imagined the whole thing. Perhaps she'd still been asleep, her nightmares blending with reality in an unexpected way. After everything that had happened, it was only natural that her imagination would take a dark turn.

But she hadn't been imagining it. She knew that now. Two days later, when her husband had determinedly seduced her, she had let him, closing her eyes to the danger because she wanted to believe, more than anything, that she was wrong.

And so now she was certain, even though she only caught glimpses of the monster behind the mask.

The demon inside her husband coveted her in some strange way. It would look at her behind Matteo's eyes, pleased when she was there. It was happiest when it was touching her—stroking her skin and tasting her body, always careful to give more pleasure than it took. And it delighted in calling her wife.

The reason why didn't occur to her straightaway. Whatever the objective of the curse had been by the person who cast it, it was different now.

Matteo was no longer wracked with pain, a prelude to his acting with murderous intent. It had lost interest in other victims. The thing inside him was solely focused on her now because it desired something else.

It wanted to breed her.

CHAPTER 20

Isobel took refuge in the conservatory, carefully checking to make sure she was alone before filling her satchel with a particular mix of herbs.

They had arrived in London a few days ago. She'd avoided intimacy with her husband by lying about the early arrival of her monthly. But now she had a plan.

Her grandmother had helped a few of the women in the village, the ones with too many mouths to feed. Helen had prepared a mixture for them that they could brew like tea. As long as the woman followed the directions properly, unwanted pregnancies could be avoided. Isobel hadn't known the exact recipe she had to follow, but it had been easy to find—the well-used volume in her grandmother's hand had several bookmarks on pages she had consulted frequently. Although, Helen had probably known the recipe by heart.

Matteo had been disappointed, but not surprised, that she hadn't fallen pregnant straightaway. He still yearned for a child, someone to live on after him in case she couldn't find a cure for his affliction. The guilt she felt at deceiving him was intense, and she constantly reminded herself that it was necessary.

In truth, her belief that the creature's intent was to breed was little more than conjecture. But nothing else could reasonably explain her present circumstances. Spirits like the one in her husband hungered for something in particular. Her reading confirmed that. Some thrived on creating chaos, others in taking the lives they could not have for themselves. But some sought a way to make their transient existence on this plane more permanent.

If she was correct and the shade inside her husband wanted to breed, then she would be endangering any child they might have. And she couldn't tell Matteo the truth, not now that she couldn't distinguish as easily between the man and the monster.

So she brewed the herbs and drank them every morning in place of tea. Then she would go downstairs and spent several hours in the library poring over her books, trying to find anything that might help them.

The small library had been sorted by subject. In addition to the books of magic and recipes for healing, there were texts on natural history, farming, and some valuable first editions of classic volumes.

The latter did not belong to Helen. They were her father's. She suspected that he had put them in the trunk for her, which made her wonder if he'd suspected that when he was gone she might need money, resources no one else knew about. The value of the books was such that, if she'd checked the trunks after his death, she might not have needed to become a governess at all.

Isobel refused to dwell on that detail, focusing on her study of the library contents instead, as well as overseeing the work in the conservatory.

The *Conte* had thankfully taken up residence in a townhouse in Mayfair, but she and Matteo stayed outside of town. The property agent had rented them a large house a scant half hour drive from London, one with a large conservatory and another midsize greenhouse farther from the main house.

A gardener had been hired to help her and Matteo with the planting of various seeds and a few cuttings for herbs—anything she thought might be useful to help him, and now herself. After the planting had been done, the gardener was reassigned to the grounds while she did the work of tending to the plants herself. And when she couldn't for whatever reason, Nino had insisted on helping.

Aside from sleeping too much, Matteo behaved very much like himself. Or at least the man she thought he was. She had to admit, there was a lot about him she didn't know—or about how the spell might have altered his normal personality. He appeared to be a dear man, conscientious and kind. If his malady hadn't succeeded in altering that, then she had to believe he was worth saving.

The thought that the spell was making him kinder and more appealing was something she dismissed right away. Based on what had happened to all those other victims, the goal had been to create a monster. She had interfered and made something else.

Though Isobel knew the demon inside him was still there, she tried her best to forget about it. Maybe it was cowardly to ignore it, but she couldn't get through her daily life unless she did. So she accepted her husband's affection and tried to treat him with the same consideration he demonstrated for her. The "other" inside him was put into a locked room in her mind, one she didn't open until she had to. Otherwise, she would go stark screaming mad.

The *Conte* visited on several occasions, and he seemed pleased with the semblance of normalcy that Matteo was able to maintain. She warned Aldo that that's all it was, a temporary reprieve, but he didn't care. He invited several of his friends over to pay calls to his son and had even gone so far as to secure them invitations to the last events of the little Season.

Isobel was nervous about mixing with others at such large social events. The calls paid to them at the country house had been stressful enough without having to worry about making small talk or dancing in a ton ballroom. But Matteo had been so taken with the idea of socializing, of being a normal man again, that she hadn't the heart to say no.

That night was going to be their first ball. Compared to the ones held during the regular Season it would be small, only a few hundred or so people. Which was a few hundred too many for Isobel. Fortunately for her, their debut in society as a couple had been delayed until she had a wardrobe befitting a rich lord's wife.

They had had to wait for the ton's most fashionable modiste, madame Josephina, to make up a new ball gown for her, as well as dresses for morning, afternoon, and evening, along with an assortment of matching pelisses. Additionally, there was a riding habit, *a la militaire* as was the fashion, and a multitude of gloves, hats, muffs, and everything else the ton deemed necessary garb for a woman to leave her house.

Her new blue day dress from Carrbridge had been immediately discarded as soon as the new purchases began to arrive. The waste bothered Isobel, but Matteo had laughed at her and told her to get used to being spoiled now that she was a future Countess.

She reluctantly abandoned her work in the library a few hours before the ball in order to get ready. The gown she was wearing was a deep emerald green velvet, with short sleeves and a full skirt.

Unlike the other fashionable gowns of the ton, it was modestly cut at the bust. Isobel didn't want to worry about falling out of her gown *and* dancing at the same time.

Her time as a governess hadn't prepared her for a ton ballroom, but she did have a little familiarity with the waltz. In her former position at Sir Isaac Warton's home, she'd accompanied the dancing master as he taught her charges in preparation for their come-out. But dancing in front of a hundred people was not the same as dancing in front of two spoiled young ladies and their bored ten-year-old brother.

Isobel put on her new gown with trepidation, dressing by herself. With an overabundance of caution, she'd decided not to employ a lady's maid. The fewer servants they had the better. She put her hair in a simple style, only slightly more elaborate than her normal coiffure. Her stays and the dress fastened in the front at her request, so she didn't need to call Matteo in to help her.

When she was done, she gave herself a long critical inspection in the bedroom looking-glass. It was still her, but different. The green set off her skin nicely and deepened the color of her eyes.

Fine feathers, she thought. Feeling slightly fraudulent, she pulled on her gloves and then smoothed her skirts.

Never in her life had she worn such a beautiful dress, not even as a child. Especially as a child, she thought, remembering the sorry state of her dresses after an afternoon rambling in the woods. She was no longer that carefree, careless girl, but the thought of spilling something on herself was enough to make her bite her nails in anxiety.

At this point, however, humiliating herself was the least of her concerns.

Matteo was waiting for her on the stairs. When he saw her coming down the steps he froze, his lips parting.

"*Cara*, you are a vision," he said, his eyes wide.

Isobel laughed despite her trepidation. "You don't have to sound so surprised," she replied cheekily, although she could feel her cheeks pinkening with pleasure.

He smiled and took her hand and spun her in a slow circle. When she faced him again, his expression was serious. "I'm afraid I can't let you go out like this. You're missing something."

She glanced down at her gown and gloves in surprise. "What am I missing? I warn you nothing else is going to fit in this gown," she said, running her hands down the tight bodice in a cursory examination.

"Well, compared to the other ladies who'll be at the party, you're nearly naked."

She scowled at him, but he just grinned at her. With a twinkle in his eye, he took a thin box from a nearby table and presented it to her with a flourish.

"What's this?" she asked.

"You can't make your debut in society without being properly attired," he said as she opened the box.

Her mouth dropped open. Nestled against the soft black interior of the box was a stunning emerald necklace and matching set of earrings. Mixed between the large oval cut emeralds were smaller glittering brown stones.

It was the most beautiful thing she had ever seen. Her first thought, after she recovered from her surprise, was that she couldn't wear it.

"I'm going to lose it," she said with a creased brow.

Matteo chuckled and took the necklace out of the box. "I assure you the clasp is very secure."

"What are these brown stones?" she asked, touching their cool smooth surface as he fastened the necklace around her neck.

"They're a variant of goldstone. I told the jeweler that I wanted something that reminded me of your eyes. I'm very pleased with the result," he said, his breath warm on the back of her neck just before he pressed a kiss there. "He's making up a matching brooch and bracelet as well, but so far only this and the earrings are ready. It was a bit of a rush job."

He removed the droplet earrings and helped her fasten them, taking advantage of the necessary proximity to press another kiss below her ear. Flushed and warm, she took the arm he extended to her and they climbed into the carriage.

Perhaps the night wouldn't be so bad after all.

CHAPTER 21

 *I*sobel smiled with gritted teeth as the rotund earl she was dancing with stepped on her feet yet again.

She really needn't have worried about her performance on the dance floor. What the dancing master should have taught her and her charges was a way to defend themselves, or more precisely their feet, from the onslaught of clumsy partners.

Foot-murdering earls aside, the night had been surprisingly pleasant. The large ballroom was impressively gilded with a multitude of crystal chandeliers. Elegantly dressed people milled about, trying not to appear to be enjoying themselves too much.

The men were more uniformly dressed in black, but the women wore a multitude of colors. She admired their jewel-like gowns from a distance, grateful that her husband's good taste ensured she was not out of place. The new jewels she wore had been universally admired. Her gown was not the only one in that particular shade of green, but it was among the most elegant.

A number of young ladies wore white, and after speaking to a few of them, she learned they were here in advance of the regular season to acquire a social polish in a less demanding and critical setting. When the regular Season commenced, their manners and looks would be evaluated and judged in the highly competitive marriage mart. The entire future of some families rested on making an advantageous match for their daughters.

It was a cutthroat business. Isobel wondered if she would have been subjected to a similar ordeal in Edinburgh had her father lived. They had never discussed giving her a season.

Turning away from her cheerless thoughts she focused on the novelty of her surroundings. In addition to the extravagantly decorated ballroom, the buffet had been lavishly laid with game, lobster patties, and other assorted delicacies. To her eyes it looked sumptuous, but she heard more than one person sniff that it was miserly compared to the buffets laid during the regular season.

The only real problem was the dancing. She suppressed a wince when her partner trod on her toes once more. Hot and winded, she was glad when the dying strains of music signaled an end to the torture. With relief, she allowed the slightly sour-smelling earl to escort her back to her party.

In addition to her husband and his father, she was surrounded by a circle of their acquaintances, friends they had made in previous visits and kept up through correspondence.

To her surprise, the circle also included family, a young cousin of Matteo's named Gideon Wells, the son of Clarence's youngest sister, Anna.

Gideon, a youth eighteen years old, was down from Oxford with some friends for the weekend. He had been thrilled to learn Matteo was in town. He had latched onto him with endearing enthusiasm and was peppering him with questions about Italy and how his cousin had met her. He gave her a commiserating smile when she rejoined the party.

"Did 'ol Lynton leave you crippled? I told my uncle it was a bad idea to accept his request for a dance," he whispered with a genial grin.

Isobel allowed herself a tiny smile in response before assuring him that she was fine. But her amusement dropped away quickly when she caught sight of her husband.

A streak of cold ran through her overheated body. Matteo's eyes were dark—too dark. And there was a tell-tale streak of black in his aura. Fighting full-blown panic, she made her way to his side and slipped a hand in his arm.

"Darling, are you feeling all right?" she asked, her voice strained.

He looked down at her, eyes glassy like dark pools reflecting distant starlight. When he didn't answer, her heart picked up speed.

"Matteo?" she whispered, caressing the inside of his arm.

"I'm fine, *mi amore*," he said, his voice as remote as the look in his eyes.

"He should be asking you that," Gideon laughed.

Matteo looked up at him sharply.

"Old Lynton stepped all over her feet. It's a good thing I already had a chance to take a turn with your lovely new wife." He leaned in as he said it, smiling at Isobel warmly.

Under her hand, Matteo stiffened and from the corner of her eye she saw his aura flare.

No, no, no!

How could she not have realized? She'd been so stupid. Normal socializing was taxing enough for Matteo, but a ball? A place where other men not only spoke to her, but also touched her. And she was obliged to let them as they partnered her on the dance floor.

Gideon kept up a steady stream of small talk, apparently not noticing that Matteo had essentially withdrawn from him and the rest of the company. She was trying to decide what to do when another man, a viscount this time, came up to their party to request a dance.

The flare-up of black next to her was startling in its intensity, and underneath her fingers she could feel him growing colder.

It must have been worse that her admirer was young and attractive. Looking up, she gave the balcony door a longing glance, ignoring the Conte's nod of approval of the viscount as an acceptable dance partner. She closed and opened her mouth, trying to come up with an appropriate excuse when rescue came from an unexpected source.

"Sorry, Berkeley, my cousin-in-law can't oblige you right now.

She's still fatigued from her last dance," Gideon said with a smile, digging in an elbow into the viscount's side and mouthing *Lynton*.

"Oh." Viscount Berkeley laughed. "Perhaps later then," he said before launching into a conversation with Gideon about the last sale at Tattersalls.

She murmured something noncommittal and turned to Matteo. "My lord, I'm a bit overheated from all this excitement. Could we take a breath of fresh air outside?"

Without waiting for an answer she tugged on his arm and led him away. Thankfully, he followed. She smiled, making polite excuses to the assembled group as they headed to the balcony. Once there, she immediately changed her mind.

Despite the coolness of the night, enough people were outside to make a stroll in the gardens inadvisable. She hailed a passing footman and asked if there was a room where they could have a little privacy.

Flustered by her boldness, the servant directed her to the empty library on the ground floor. Trying to appear sanguine and composed, she hurried into the darkened room, pulling Matteo in after her.

He turned her around, his grip tight, before she could find a taper to light. There was, however, enough moonlight filtering through the glass doors leading to the garden to make out most of the room, including the man in front of her and his intense expression.

"Did Lynton hurt you?" Matteo asked, his voice reverberating with that strange oscillation she'd grown to fear.

But this was not about her feelings. It was about distracting the demon from harmful intent.

"No!" She assured him hastily. Her fingers trembled as she reached up to stroke his face. "I just wanted to be alone with you," she whispered, tugging on his cravat to pull him down for a kiss.

That was all it took.

Matteo's arms wrapped around her, his hands rough and searching. His mouth aggressively plundered hers as they stood there in near darkness. Yanking down her sleeves he exposed her breasts and she gasped, wondering what she had done.

His hands cupped her before he bent and his mouth closed over one rapidly hardening peak.

She began to have trouble standing as he sucked hard on one breast and then the other, his tongue leaving a trail between them. She was about to put her hands around his neck when she heard it, that distinctive purring growl no normal man would ever make.

Her entire body clenched in both fear and arousal.

"My lord?" she asked apprehensively.

He didn't answer. Instead, he lifted and carried her deeper into the room. There was no couch in the library, only armchairs, so he set her down on a sturdy looking waist high cabinet in the far corner just outside the light of the glass doors.

Breath a little ragged, she tentatively opened her arms as he pulled her to him. Closing a fist in her hair, he tugged her head to the side, exposing her neck so his mouth could work its way down to her breast. His other hand moved under her skirt, tugging it upward before pushing her legs open.

His fingers were cold as they stroked her intimately, but they warmed quickly, almost as if she was transferring her heat to him. He growled again and tore at his breeches before pulling her to him with hard hands.

Isobel's lips parted and she threw back her head as he roughly brought their bodies together. A sound escaped her, a cross between a moan and a whimper as his shaft worked all the way inside her tight wet channel.

The shade inside Matteo liked the noise she made. It purred in approval and withdrew before pumping back into her forcefully.

It's okay, he's warm, he's warm, she repeated to herself, even though she knew it wasn't true.

Putting her hands on his shoulders, she held on as he rocked into her body. His hands held her tight against him while he took her mouth hungrily, his tongue mimicking the movements and rhythm of his shaft as he penetrated her again and again.

Around her, the room spun. It felt as if her will was being torn from its moorings as her husband's large and hard cock plundered and consumed with an intensity not his own. She wouldn't think about her body's soft and eager acceptance just now. The shame would come later.

The sudden burning orgasm that coursed through her over-whelmed her senses, making her blind and deaf as her body went rigid, convulsing in his arms...which was why she didn't hear the door open.

A sharp exhalation escaped her as male laughter penetrated her lethargy. At least two men had entered the room. For the moment they were shielded by the deeper shadows at the back of the room, but the men were moving closer. If they lit a taper she and Matteo would be seen.

With trembling hands, she clutched at him, but it was as if he didn't hear them. He didn't stop making love to her, continuing to move in and out her body with determined thrusts. She tugged on his hair, trying to signal him to stop as the men moved closer, but he was insensible.

A startling pulse of pleasure streaked through her as the men stepped into view, laughing as one handed the other a cigar. Despite having just climaxed, her body tightened hungrily around Matteo's thick member as he relentlessly claimed her warm wet sheath.

Heart in her throat, she put both her hands on Matteo's mouth, holding her breath when one spoke to the other.

"We better smoke these outside, or I'll never hear the end of it from my wife," the man said.

It was their host, Lord Southmont.

The other man said something she didn't catch while Southmont opened the door. Tense in Matteo's arms, she belatedly noticed he had stopped moving too. Frozen together in their intimate embrace they stayed silent in the shadows just a few feet away from discovery.

The men, distracted by their own conversation, went out with their cigars and disappeared into the garden.

Isobel let out a shaky breath, her body slumping against Matteo in exhausted relief. But he was still hard inside her...and he wasn't finished.

He put his hands on either side of her face and took her mouth again before slipping out of her. Languorous in his hold, she barely registered when he hauled her off the cabinet and turned her away from him.

For a moment his hands moved over her, stroking her bared breasts and down to the heated core under her skirts while he drew on her neck with his lips. Enervated by his touch she leaned against him until his hand forced her head down, bending her over the cabinet.

Startled, she clung to the polished wood surface as the head of him circled her heated entrance. One of his feet nudged her legs farther apart and then he was inside, so large he was almost too much for her. Stroking fast, he drove deeply into her, making her cry out. She pressed her cheek against the cabinet's surface, trying to hold on as her body moved helplessly underneath him. But he wasn't satisfied with her just holding on. He took hold of her breasts and pinched the tips until she bucked and cried out, blinded by another climax.

A few moments more and a shudder passed through him, his breath ragged and low when he whispered. "I love you, Isabella."

She shuddered too...because it wasn't Matteo speaking to her. It was the demon.

CHAPTER 22

If the cursed has moments of lucidity, moments when he or she goes about their business, their normal life and work, then the possibility of purging the taint remains. If the cursed is overwhelmed by the demon spirit inside them for all or most of the day, then the cursed should be relieved of their burden.

Isobel clutched the thin volume, pressing it so hard against her body that it dug into her ribs. It wasn't one of the books her grandmother had written. The diary was much older and written in a masculine hand. It had been in the last trunk, a forgotten little leather bound journal that didn't identify its author. It was also in Greek, a language her father had taught her along with Latin, French, and a little Italian.

The brief passage was the clearest mention of a spell that resembled what was happening to Matteo. She had found others, descriptions of curses that instructed the user on how to afflict others with ailments from a mild rash to sexual dysfunction. Other more pernicious curses made a person insensible, while a few killed.

What she'd found related to Matteo's condition was vague. She didn't know what the book meant by a purge. Despite translating all of the text in the book, there wasn't more detail on that part. But now that she knew what she was looking for, maybe things would go faster. And she still had more volumes to check.

She had asked the *Conte* to acquire several more that had been mentioned in her reading through one of his agents in town. He had sent word that they had been found, and he would drop them off this afternoon. Pleased that the count was finally contributing to his son's recovery, she was actually looking forward to his visit for a change.

Unfortunately, her assumption that Aldo was going to be helpful proved false. A few hours later he'd burst into the library, tracking mud on the carpet all the way up to the table she'd been sitting at, making notes on her reading. He'd been looking for Matteo, but his son had been asleep...again.

When she told the count they could no longer attend any of the upcoming balls left in the season—without saying explicitly why—he'd dismissed her concerns and argued with her. Aldo had no idea how close his son had come to losing control on the night of the ball.

The *Conte* only saw what he wanted to see. "You're overreacting! Matteo was having a fine time at the ball until you dragged him home early. And it's your behavior you should be concerned with, young lady."

Her chin rose. "And just what does that mean?" she asked, close to losing her temper.

"My friend, Ridgeley, saw the two of you leaving the library. Your very first ball and you can't behave with even the slightest bit of decency and decorum," he said coldly.

She looked up, her lips parting in indignation.

"I knew letting Matteo marry so far beneath him would be a big mistake," Aldo added with a sneer. "All of my friends were whispering about the two of you and what you had been doing."

Isobel's face flamed, but she stood up from her chair. She placed her palms flat on the table and glared. "I did what I had to do to keep your son from killing anyone."

The *Conte* scoffed, and she gritted her teeth.

"How dare you criticize me," she hissed. "I did what I had to do to keep him from having another one of his spells right there on the

129

dance floor. As far as I'm concerned, all of your precious friends owe their lives to me. How did you think he was going to react when I danced with other men? Did you think the thing inside him would tolerate their hands on me?"

Aldo stopped and stared at her, the surprise and dismay clear on his face.

"It doesn't work like that," he said, denial writ large on his face.

"Well, it works like that now," she said hoarsely.

They glared at each other until eventually the count looked away. "I will make your excuses at the Wilmot's tonight," he said eventually. "And whatever else involves dancing. The little Season is almost over in any case."

Isobel sat down, tired. There was silence for a long minute. She knew she had nothing to be ashamed of, but it was difficult to maintain her composure knowing the events in the library were probably public knowledge.

What did their host think? Had Southmont realized he'd been in the library at the same time?

"This is for you," Aldo said, taking an envelope from his breast pocket and sliding it toward her. "It's a letter. From Clarence's ward, Amelia. There is another for Matteo from his cousin Martin."

Heartened, Isobel took the envelope and pressed it to her breast.

It was a timely reminder of why she was doing this. Matteo was as innocent as those children. In the little time she'd had with him, he had demonstrated nothing but a conscientious regard for her and other people.

He was everything Aldo was not. If she had to suffer a few scandalized whispers to preserve that, it did not signify.

"Thank you," she replied quietly before going to wake her husband for lunch.

A FEW DAYS LATER, Isobel was working in the conservatory. She was tending to the seedlings that had managed to sprout in their little pots as well as checking her store of powders and chemicals she'd acquired from local London apothecaries.

She checked the same drawer repeatedly, as if the contents would suddenly reappear out of thin air. But she couldn't magically regenerate the dried leola root she used in her morning infusion to prevent pregnancy. The cutting she had planted had failed to sprout, and discreet inquiries to the local apothecary confirmed that the root wasn't commonly used here in London.

The apothecary sent her a substitute, one he assured her would work the same way. She had little choice but to believe him.

"*Cara*, are you in here?"

With a guilty start, Isobel turned to face Matteo. He'd been out riding with Nino and Ottavio that morning. The older servant trailed him inside, looking closely at the rows and rows of pots covering the nearby tables while Ottavio loitered near the door.

She was relieved to see Matteo up and active. These days he slept long into the morning. He only roused when she woke him, coaxing him out of bed with effort. Once he was up he seemed fine, but there had been a few mornings when she'd doubted he would wake at all. It frightened her, and she worried that the curse was working itself deeper into him.

"Did you enjoy your ride?" she asked, picking up a seedling pot as Matteo reached her.

"Yes. Did you enjoy your flowers?" he asked quietly.

Puzzled, she looked up. "What flowers?"

"The ones in the foyer. Gideon sent them. He's back in town...and he's sending flowers to my wife."

Too late, Isobel noticed the extra vibration in Matteo's deceptively soft voice. She put down the pot on her worktable.

"Is he? I hadn't seen them," she said lightly.

"Have you seen him?" he asked, leaning on the nearest table.

She laughed. "No, of course not. A young blood of the ton is out at races and boxing matches. He doesn't bother paying calls—even to his relations. He sends flowers instead, a simple courtesy."

By the end of her speech, she was struggling to keep her tone even.

Matteo's cold fingers wrapped around the back of her neck, his fingers drifting into the hair at the base of her skull. "And you would never lie to me, would you, Isabella?"

"No," she whispered, her throat tight.

His expression softened incrementally. "I know that," he said, his intense gaze taking in every inch of her face before he kissed her.

The coolness of his lips was startling in the warmth of the conservatory. She shivered despite the sudden rush of heat that coursed through her body. When his mouth moved down to her neck he began to undo the ties in the front of her bodice. He pulled her closer, yanking the front of her dress down so hard a seam popped.

Startled, she opened her eyes briefly, peeking over his shoulder.

"My lord, wait," she said urgently, trying to hold the top of her gown up.

Matteo hadn't waited to dismiss the guards.

But he wasn't listening to her. He moved down her body to kneel in front her, pushing her skirts out of his way as he went. Trying to hold up her bodice with one hand, she urged him away with the other. But he took hold of her wrist in an iron grip before backing her against the glass wall of the conservatory.

She gasped as the bare skin of her back made contact with the cold slick wall, and Matteo responding in kind, growling as he hooked one of her legs over his shoulder, exposing her to his mouth——and the eyes of the men.

Blood pumping loudly in her ears, she looked up to see Nino making a rapid exit, but Ottavio was standing there...watching from behind the hydrangea bushes.

Matteo's bulk concealed her most intimate place, but the servant could likely see her bare legs and what skin was exposed by the torn bodice.

"*Matteo!*" she cried, but he paid her no attention.

He was too intent on his task. His tongue and fingers were exploring her intimate flesh, opening and softening her for his inevitable claiming.

Frantically she waved at Ottavio, trying to signal him to go away.

If Matteo came to his senses long enough to look behind him, he would lose control.

But the asinine servant wouldn't move. His avaricious stare was taking in everything, then one hand thrust into his trousers to rub himself through his clothing.

She couldn't shout at him to leave. If she did, it would sign the fool's death warrant. Lips clamped firmly shut, she tried to shift her skirts out of Matteo's grip enough to throw them over him. She was only partially successful, but it had to be enough. Her focus and strength were waning as her soft wet channel was alternately filled by his fingers and tongue in a rhythmic, coordinated invasion. Working in a second finger into her sheath, he grazed the pearl of her sex with his teeth before biting down gently.

Isobel was no match for the sensual onslaught. Her bodice fell forward as she put one hand on Matteo's head and clutched at the glass behind her for support. Her nipples peaked in contact with the air, but she couldn't cover herself. A sharp pulsing pleasure robbed her of strength. Nearly falling forward only deepened Matteo's penetration as he consumed her with abandon.

Throughout the encounter, she could feel Ottavio's eyes on her. She tried not to look directly at him, but when the orgasm crashed through her, her eyes flew open. Her gaze locked with his as the spasms racked her body, an involuntary cry escaping her lips.

Her vision blurred as she slumped against the wall. The sight of her—breasts exposed, skin damp and hot from climax—proved too much for the lustful servant. He tore open his breeches, exposing his large engorged member and pumping it hard. Repelled, Isobel squeezed her eyes shut and dug her fingers into her demon husband's back.

Matteo took it as a signal to move. His hands cupped her bottom, pulling her up until she was suspended in his arms, her legs wrapped around his waist.

It was as if she weighed nothing. Overwhelmed by the power the smooth controlled motion betrayed, she held what little breath she had left for an endless moment before he plunged inside her.

She moaned loudly, throwing her head back. Her body was no longer under her control. She moved up and down helplessly as *it* willed, an eager recipient for every thrust, bite, and hot sucking kiss.

It was the same as the incident in the library. She was simply carried along, her pleasure the demon's only goal. Like a true incubus, all it wanted was her surrender.

So she gave it to him.

His hands were busy, one roughly moving up over her breasts and down her waist. Meanwhile, the fingers of the one supporting her stroked the smooth skin of her bottom until one worked into the forbidden little nether hole, making her scream aloud at the unexpected invasion.

She clutched hard at Matteo's hair as a dark wave of pleasure rose and crashed over her, but his tempo didn't waver. He continued to piston in and out, her spasming channel gripping him tightly as he rocked her against the cold glass.

Her scream of completion was still ringing in her ears when Matteo turned his head enough to take one of her hands into his mouth. He nipped at her fingers before he began to suck them. His tongue caressed each in turn before drawing on them hard, sending a streak of fire straight into her sex. Trembling violently, Isobel pulled her hand away and tugged his head down to her neck.

He obliged her by sucking and biting at the tender skin there, the pain mingling with pleasure to create an alien state of euphoria that was probably another climax, a long slow burning that took as much as it gave. This one stole her vision, as if she'd been staring at the sun too long.

Lost in abandon, her head lolled weakly until it came to rest on Matteo's shoulder. Barely able to see, she glanced past him, too weak to react when she saw Ottavio. She had forgotten about him. He was still there…looking spent.

Isabel shut her eyes tightly, burying her face in the crease of Matteo's neck. Distantly, she heard him shout. His cock jerked inside her and his seed coated her womb in hot bursts.

Time was unimportant in the dark. She felt movement, warm skin against hers, things hard and soft—but the ability to distinguish between them was gone. Everything—every object, every texture—blended into the next.

She didn't open her eyes for a long time. When she did, she was cradled in Matteo's lap, his concerned brown eyes looking down at her in surprise. Listless, she reached up to touch his cheek, dropping it when the now warm bristled surface proved too much for her hyper-sensitive skin.

Turning her head, she looked at the empty room around them. They were alone.

CHAPTER 23

$\mathcal{M}$atteo's memories of what happened in the conservatory were confused, to say the least.

Isobel had been surprised that he recalled anything at all. His memory of their wedding night was clear enough, but she attributed that to his being normal at the start. However, he hadn't mentioned what had happened in the library at the Southmont's ball at all.

But now he remembered his anger and jealousy over Gideon's flowers, how they had overwhelmed him until they were catalyzed into lust. The rest was in bits and pieces...which was more than enough.

He was racked by guilt. He kept apologizing and casting her tormented glances whenever they happened to be alone together. It was decidedly inconvenient, considering all she wanted was to forget the incident.

Isobel didn't blame herself for succumbing to his demands. What she didn't want to think about was how much she enjoyed it. Not that her body let her forget. She would be working in the library when a snippet of memory would intrude into her thoughts, overwhelming her with heat and sending a pulse of forbidden pleasure through her. The unexpected arousal was uncomfortable and embarrassing.

She could barely look Niko in the eye and avoided Ottavio at all costs. Luckily, he spent most of his time with Matteo, who at this moment was mostly avoiding her too.

The thought of making an excuse to dismiss the younger servant crossed her mind more than once. However, there was nothing she could think of that was sufficient grounds for dismissal, yet benign enough to avoid sending Matteo into another fit.

Torn, she decided the only thing she could do was keep her silence.

Avoiding the issue had at least one important benefit. By throwing herself into her research, she made real progress in formulating a ritual to purge the curse.

In the end, Isobel had decided to combine aspects of several spells and rituals found in the books. There wasn't actually much of a choice. No one account matched exactly what she had seen or was living with. Which was why the possibility she might be dealing with two distinct realities occurred to her.

The books included a number of references to possession. While each was different, they all shared some similarities. The subject rarely remembered what they did when under the influence and often their bodies would either be very cold or very hot.

Their actions varied widely, but as far as she could tell once that action had been carried out—be it murder, theft, or sex—then the cursed person would recover themselves…for a time.

Eventually, the cursed would degenerate in some way and usually grow weak or mad. Then they would die, if they hadn't been killed already. The process could take months or even years.

Some of the stories attributed the possession to a specific spirit or demon, giving it a name. She didn't disagree with the practice. What she'd experienced made her believe there was an intelligence behind what was happening. She had seen it herself, felt it watching her. But it wasn't a *real* demon.

After reading everything on hand, she knew that if it was a genuine demon, the death and destruction it caused would have been far greater. But there was no better name for what she had seen, so a demon it remained in her mind…or rather two demons.

Her belief that Matteo had been cursed intentionally was now cemented as a certainty. Something truly terrible had been called and then cast inside him.

Flashes of that night at Sir Clarence's estate skittered through her mind. The demon hadn't been able to kill her so it had been prepared to hurt her in any way it could. However, she now believed that demon was gone, burned up in the black shadow in that god-forsaken cottage. Her actions had probably destroyed it.

It had been sheer blind luck. But in her ignorance she'd left Matteo open and exposed. The damage to his aura had been severe and without its protection, something else had found him an easy host. This other entity had different needs and desires, but it had the potential for equal destruction. Or it might if its attention finally moved away from her.

Incubus.

The name echoed in her mind. She'd used it before, but now really believed that was what she was dealing with. Even if it had been accidental, she had been the one to let it in. Its singular focus on her may have had a lot to do with that.

And if the accounts she'd been studying were accurate, the fact that Matteo was starting to remember what he did when under the demon's control wasn't a hopeful sign as she'd initially thought.

It was a warning that she was running out of time.

CHAPTER 24

*L*ate that afternoon, Isobel finally went back into the conservatory. She had given Nino instructions to care for the plants for the last few days because she hadn't been able to face going back inside. Every time she had tried it felt as if she was about to burst into flames of embarrassment. He had followed her instructions without question, but his carefully controlled expression spoke volumes.

However, it was past time she got a hold of herself. She needed to check on the plants and other stores, to see if all of the ingredients the ritual required were at hand. In reality, she knew getting the recipe right was the least of her concerns. The real work of the ritual rested almost entirely on her shoulders. But the mixture of herbs was one aspect she could control now, so that's what she was going to do.

Isobel spent at least an hour on her inventory. To her relief, she appeared to have most of the basic ingredients she needed. The one issue was the last component, yarrow, for purification. But the seeds she'd acquired from the apothecary had sprouted, so she busied herself with transferring the small seedlings to bigger pots.

Footsteps signaled the approach of her husband. She looked up eagerly, despite her trepidation over having yet another uncomfortable conversation about how sorry he was.

Except it wasn't him. It was Ottavio, and he was closing the doors leading back into the house.

Perfect. This was just what she needed. But perhaps something was wrong.

"Is everything all right?" she called out in her heavily accented Italian. "Does his lordship need me?"

Ottavio waited until he was just a few feet away then shook his head. "It sleeps," he said, his voice coarse unlike the other Italians she was surrounded with.

Chagrined, she didn't look up at him directly until he came to stand next to her. Glancing up at his face, she stilled. The way he was smiling at her was far too familiar.

The presentiment of danger struck her a second too late. He grabbed her by the arms, making her drop the clay pot she was holding. Dragging her to him effortlessly, his mouth came down on hers before she could move.

Isobel twisted her head violently away.

"What are you doing? Stop!" she yelled, trying to push him away.

But he was too strong. He was one of the largest men she'd ever seen, taller and broader than Matteo and at least sixteen stone. His bulk blocked out sight of the door, enveloping her like a blanket of sweaty flesh. Disgusted, she struggled, throwing all of her weight to the side in an effort to break his hold.

"Be quiet," he hissed before wrapping an arm around her waist. The other began to tug at her bodice. None of her efforts to get loose made the slightest difference. He bent to whisper in her ear. "I know you want me. I saw it in your eyes when the beast was fucking you. You wanted me to watch. Don't worry, I can satisfy you much better than him. You deserve a real man..."

He pressed her against his body, grinding his pelvis into her. He was already hard, his body heat smothering her.

Isobel gulped air, her heart pounding violently. "No! I don't want this, and I didn't want you to watch," Isobel cried. "If I had said anything Matteo would have killed you. And he's not a beast! It's not his fault. Now let go of me!"

Ottavio stared at her angrily and didn't let go. Instead, he grabbed her hair, nearly pulling it out of the roots as he yanked her toward him.

"*Strega puttana*, you can't believe that. It's a monster, and it should be destroyed. And it will be soon, and then where will you be? The *Conte* will get rid of you as soon as he's gone! Nothing save an heir will help you...and we both know that's not going to happen."

Isobel went white. "What the hell are you talking about?"

The brute sneered. "I know all about your little potion, the one you drink every morning. You won't risk giving the monster a babe. And I don't blame you. But only a babe will save you from Aldo. So don't be a fool. I'll put a babe in you and you'll let me, *maledetta strega*."

He yanked on her hair again, pulling her face in close to lick her neck and ear.

"Oh, God," she whispered tearfully, her heart sinking in her chest.

How did he know all of that? She'd always thought Ottavio was slow because he rarely spoke, but if he'd managed to learn all of those things then she'd severely underestimated him. What if he told Matteo? Or the Count? If she lost his son in the purge, he wouldn't hesitate to get rid of her.

Too focused on supernatural dangers, she'd overlooked the human ones. But that didn't mean she was going to submit to Ottavio. There was no way in hell.

"I will not let you blackmail me!" She twisted in his grasp, bringing up a hand to rake his face with her nails.

He swore and let go of her, his face purple with anger. She'd only managed to get a few steps away before he rushed forward. He struck out with one meaty fist.

It was a glancing blow, not landing with his full weight, but it was more than enough. The stroke sent her crashing to the ground, her lip bleeding.

Isobel landing on her back, hitting the ground with enough force to knock her breathless.

Ottavio towered over her. *"Maiala lercia!* Do you think you're better than me? You're only here because you're a witch—but you were a servant just like me," he shouted.

Isobel cringed, crawling backward.

His beady eyes glinted with malevolence. "I'll show you, you're no better," he growled as if to himself as he tore open his breeches.

She only caught a glimpse of his red angry staff before he was on top of her, crushing her down into the floor of the conservatory. He was tearing at her clothes and forcing open her legs.

It was just like before. A black flood of memory rose up, throwing up images she'd buried in the deepest recesses of her mind. She sobbed aloud, only to be struck in the mouth, his rough large hand covering her nose and mouth as he tried to move between her kicking legs.

Isobel couldn't breathe. Panic tainted her vision black at the edges, so she did the only thing she could think of.

She used her power again. Just like before...but completely different.

There was no *other* living inside of Ottavio. There was just him— his small mean soul. With a white-hot anger and a considerable amount of fear, she reached out with her ability.

This time it was easier to take hold of it, but she couldn't just push him away. His soul was anchored too strongly. She tore at it, squeezing with all her strength. When that didn't loosen his hold she passed raw power through him like a bolt of lighting.

Above her, Ottavio stopped moving. He gave one sharp jerk, a whole-body convulsion before looking down at her in disbelief, his expression growing waxy and wooden.

They stayed frozen in that violent tableau for what felt like an eternity, but it must have only been a second before an inhuman roar filled the air. The heavy body of her assaulter was removed and swung up in the air like a rag doll.

Isobel scrambled back, eyes wide in horrified disbelief. Her hand stung as it landed on something sharp, but she barely registered the pain.

The thing holding Ottavio by the neck wasn't Matteo or the shade hiding behind him, peeking at her lustfully. This was the demon, unfiltered and in control.

The blackness of its aura covered her husband from head to toe, darker than midnight. Its eyes were holes cut into another world, a place that she would have nightmares about for years to come. And it was howling, its face contorted into a rabid mask, one so thin it couldn't hide what it truly was.

The heavy thud of Ottavio's body hitting the floor made her flinch. The demon fell on him, still screaming with that awful rending sound. It grabbed the larger man's head, lifted it, and slammed it back into the ground over and over.

Her screams joined the demon's as it pounded the dead servant's head into pulp. There was blood everywhere and bits of skull and brain smeared all around them like a halo. Isobel shut her eyes, screaming and sobbing, trying to block out the noise by putting her hands over her ears.

Everything went quiet abruptly. Isobel opened her eyes to see Matteo in a fighting stance standing in front of her protectively.

Behind him near the door of the conservatory was Nino. He was holding a hunting rifle on the demon. His face was grey and he was shaking, but the gun he held was steady enough.

"Don't, my lord," she whispered.

The demon cocked his ear in her direction but didn't turn to face her.

"This is your fault!" Nino shouted in English, catching her full attention. He wasn't talking to her, however. "This is what happens when you treat your woman like a whore, taking her with no regard to the eyes watching. You make other men covet her. And because you treat her like a whore, others think they can too."

The demon growled something unintelligible. It almost sounded like *wife*.

When he made a move toward Nino, she cried out to him to wait. "Matteo, please help me," she said, holding out a hand to him.

To her surprise, it was covered in blood. She'd cut it open on a broken pottery shard from the pot Ottavio made her drop.

It glanced her way, but when it saw the blood its face changed, softening. It rushed forward, grabbing her hand. When the blood made contact with his skin he rocked back, letting go. There was something like mist in her eyes for a moment, obscuring her view of his face but when she blinked it was gone. And then Matteo was there, looking down at her and himself in dismay.

"Isabella, are you all right?" he asked hoarsely, reaching down for her.

Isobel scooted away from him. It was instinctive. His face fell, and she looked away.

"*Signora.* I believe that cut will require a needle and thread. I can sew you up."

It was Nino. He had come up behind them when the demon departed, but he still held the hunting piece protectively in front of him. He did, however, keep the barrel pointed down.

She glanced at the cut. It wasn't flowing freely anymore, but cleaning would surely open it again. Pushing herself up with her other hand, she stood and nodded at Nino, studiously avoiding looking at Matteo or the carnage behind him.

Once she had regained her feet, she swayed slightly. Both Matteo and Nino rushed to help her, but she waved them away. She didn't want anyone to touch her right now.

"I'm all right," she said in a low voice.

Nino extended his arm, gesturing to the door. She followed him out, leaving Matteo alone to clean up the mess.

CHAPTER 25

*I*sobel's eye twitched as the needle passed through the flesh of her palm. She had washed it out herself, then poured strong spirits over the cut.

It had hurt like hell. The cut was quite deep. After Nino finished sewing it closed, she would bind her hand with a poultice of her grandmother's design. But first she needed to get through the stitching.

They were in the library, sitting at the table nearest the sideboard where they kept the spirits.

"It might help if you drank some of that brandy, instead of just using it as an antiseptic," Nino murmured.

Her lip twitched involuntarily. It actually sounded like a great idea. Pouring with her free hand, she raised the glass, but her hand was shaking so badly she spilled most of it on her bodice.

She looked down at the torn morning dress. "Doesn't matter. I'm going to burn this anyway."

Nino paused to hand her a towel. Isobel looked at it, confused.

"For your lip. It's bleeding again too."

"Oh," she said softly, taking the cloth and holding it to her mouth.

Nino ducked his head. "*Signora*, I want to apologize. About Ottavio. I should have done something."

"It wasn't your fault."

"I think it was, actually." He looked away. "He'd been talking, complaining. This job wasn't what he expected. The *Conte* hired him for his strength and size. Everyone assumed he was stupid, and he hated it. He was accustomed to getting his fill of female attention too, but here in England he couldn't even speak to them. I should have realized he'd start looking your way and...circumstances being what they are, he got ideas."

Isobel shook her head. "It still wasn't your fault. There are a dozen things I could have said and done to prevent this as well. One of them might have worked—or none of them."

Nino sniffed, but he nodded, anyway. "I think this should do it," he said, tying a knot at the end of the thread.

He did fine work. The stitching was neat and narrow.

"How often have you done this?"

"A few times," he said, cleaning up the sewing materials from the table. "Would you like some comfrey?"

Surprised, she looked up. "I was not aware that you knew anything about healing plants."

"I've been paying attention," he said dismissively.

She picked up the glass again and took a large sip. The brandy burned her throat, and her eyes watered.

"Actually I made a salve that will work better. It's in the conservatory with the other supplies," she said, wincing at the taste of the brandy.

She'd only ever drunk wine and that had usually been watered down. No matter how expensive this brandy was—and if Matteo had bought it, then it was very costly—it still tasted like a combustible solvent going down her throat.

"I'll go fetch it. And then I'll help his lordship clean in there."

Swallowing hard, she nodded as he made his way to the door.

He paused at the threshold. "It's different now, isn't it?"

Taking another bracing sip, she squinted up at him. "What do you mean?"

"The beast. It doesn't kill the same way. Before all it had to do was touch someone and they died. Now it uses its strength to beat you to death. That and the way it behaves with you."

Too tired for explanations, Isobel dismissed his comment with a shrug. All she wanted was a bath. She would worry about everything else later.

HOURS LATER, Matteo walked into Isobel's bedroom. It had taken a long time to dig a hole deep enough for the bastard's body.

It was a macabre bit of irony. Usually Ottavio was the one digging the hole. Nino had complained that it usually went a lot faster, but Matteo refused to apologize—despite how he felt.

It had been upsetting. He'd never had to bury one of his victims before. That was done out of his sight on orders from his father. This was also the first death he remembered clearly.

He wanted to say that he would regret it. The violence and the carnage would stay with him for a long time. But he wasn't sorry that the *figlio di mignotta* was dead.

Isobel was sitting at her dressing table in her nightgown. She was examining her bruised lip by candlelight in the looking glass. He came up behind her, their eyes meeting in the glass. Tentatively, he put his hands on her shoulders. To his relief, she didn't flinch away.

"I'm sorry you had to see that," he whispered. "I never wanted to do something like that in front of you.

Under his hand, Isobel's shoulders shook as she took a deep shuddering breath. "That wasn't you. Trust me, that was very clear."

He didn't know what to say. Well, there was one thing...

"It felt like me," he whispered. "And perhaps there is a reason for that."

She turned around to face him. "What do you mean?"

Passing a hand over his face, he chose his words carefully. "I mean that I would have killed him too, curse or no curse. He was hurting you, trying to rape you." He closed his eyes, hands fisting as the rage welled up again. "Nino was right. It was my fault."

"*Again*, that's not true."

His Isabella was getting angry, and it touched him. Even after everything he'd done to her, she was trying to absolve him of guilt. She didn't understand.

"Yes, it is. Every terrible thing that has happened to you is because of me. And as badly as I felt about that, I wasn't truly sorry because I was able to keep you. You're my wife, and I would protect you with my life...and now I know I would kill for you too. I would do whatever I have to do to keep you safe. But *I'm* the one you need to be protected from."

He looked down at his hands. They were clean now, but he could still see the blood on them. "Isabella, I think it's time to end this. It's time for me to die."

Her brow creased and her shoulders slumped. She looked so exhausted. "*No.*"

He began to argue with her, but she forestalled him with a hand, her injured one. "No. It is not time for you to die. I'm not ready to give up—and you didn't kill Ottavio. I did."

Dropping to one knee he took her hand. "Isabella, you don't have to lie to spare my feelings. I remember everything I did. This time the memories are as clear as if they were my own."

Her hazel eyes stared at him seriously. "I know that, but you failed to grasp one important detail. The man you pulled off me and beat until his head split open was *already* dead." She looked away. "I guess I learned from my experience with your demon. I didn't mean to kill him. Not at first."

He wasn't aware that he was gaping at her until she leaned over and pushed his mouth closed with a delicate white finger under his chin.

"Are you sure?" he whispered.

"Yes," she nodded slowly and reached for his hand. "Come lie down with me. I want you to hold me."

He bowed his head, his forehead touching hers. How is it she always managed to undo him so easily?

"Anything. Anything you want."

With a hand on his cheek, she drew away from him and gave him a small sad smile. "I want you to live."

Her words hit him like a body blow, making it hard to catch his breath. But his witch didn't give him time to dwell. She took his arm and led him to the bed. They lay down together, and she curled against his chest. There was nothing sexual about their embrace this time. It was about comfort.

"It was awful, what it did," she said eventually.

"What *I* did."

"No, what *it* did. I—I may have found a way to be rid of it. Possibly. I've been improvising, adapting a ritual that will cure you. It involves a purge and a cleansing fire. The curse needs to be burned away at the root and your aura sealed so nothing gets back in."

Matteo tensed. Isobel peeked up at him from underneath her lashes, her skin almost luminescent in the afternoon light. Slowly she stroked his chest with her pale white fingers.

"That's wonderful news *mi tesoro*."

Her hand fisted in his shirt. "It will be very painful. More painful than you can possibly imagine. And if I do it wrong, you may not survive." She snorted slightly. "I *do* want you to live, more than anything. But I might be the one killing you after all."

He squeezed her tighter. "If that's my fate, I accept it. I'll never be anything but grateful to you."

Isobel rested her head on his chest. "I don't want your gratitude. I just want you."

Despite everything that had just occurred, the world was suddenly a bit brighter.

"Well, thank you anyway...for letting me love you. Even if it's just for a little while."

BEING secretive was becoming second nature to Isobel.

She kept Matteo out of the ritual preparation, despite his insistence on helping. Though she believed that the demon couldn't know what it didn't witness, the deeper integration of the incubus into the fabric of his being was worrisome. She had no way of knowing how intelligent it was and didn't want to take any chances on alerting it to their plans. It knew too much already.

But she now knew something about it too. While it enjoyed her body, it abhorred her blood. It had reacted badly when it came into contact with a few drops after the attack in the conservatory. Either it had been driven away by some property in the blood, or the blood had hurt it in some way.

Which was why she was altering the ritual and not telling Matteo. If he knew the true extent of the danger, he would never cooperate.

It was something her grandmother had told her once. Blood magic meant sacrifice, sometimes your own. Adding her blood to the ritual tied her to it inextricably. If she couldn't control the fire in the purge, it wouldn't just consume Matteo. It would claim her too...

The *Conte* was being kept in the dark, as well. Matteo was his only heir and in spite of his pompousness and selfishness, the man did love his son.

If Aldo saw Matteo in pain, he would interfere and jeopardize all of their work. For this reason, Isobel decided not to confide in Nino either, even though she would have appreciated his assistance. However, when it came right down to it, she didn't know if his regard for her was enough to overcome his loyalty to his employer.

She was alone in this.

At least that's something you're used to.

CHAPTER 26

A hand on Matteo's forehead roused him from a deep sleep. It always took him so long to wake, even though he knew it was Isobel doing the waking. It was always her. No one else ever dared to touch him.

Surfacing from sleep, he looked up at her. She was wearing his favorite day dress, a green muslin that matched the color of her eyes. It was a simple gown, modestly cut, and it always made him want to make love to her. Not the frenzied intercourse when the demon was in control, but a slow sweet joining. Something human. That wasn't possible anymore.

If he wanted Isobel, *it* always came, eager to touch her too. Even now that he was starting to remember the experiences, to feel them as his own, it was like he was spinning out of control—a mere observer of the play. So he'd stopped asking Isobel for his husbandly rights. It wasn't fair to her when the demon already demanded so much.

His wife leaned over him, pressing a soft kiss to his lips. She never did that.

"What's wrong?" he asked, sitting up.

The tiniest smirk betrayed her before her countenance sobered.

"It's time, Matteo."

"Oh." His head suddenly felt like it was filling with air. He gave himself a hard shake before following her out of bed. Regaining his equilibrium, he put on his boots. "I had no idea that you were so close to being ready."

"I thought it better to surprise you, in case..."

She didn't need to finish.

Nodding, he followed her out of the room. Once in the hallway, she gestured for him to head down the stairs. On the other side of the windows the light was already fading, which meant he'd slept most of the day away. Again.

At the foyer, he hesitated. Had she prepared the ritual in the library or the conservatory? It made more sense to use the conservatory since the ritual was supposed to use fire, but he hated going in there now, and Isobel must despise it.

"Where are we going?" he asked when Isobel led him past the entrance to the library and down the hallway to the kitchen.

There was no one there. They didn't have many staff, but the few they did have always congregated in the kitchen. If nothing else, Cook was a fixture there. But the kitchen was still and dark, the hearth cold. He found it disquieting.

"I gave the entire staff the night off," she said belatedly before opening the back door.

A blast of icy wind greeted them. It was bitingly cold outside, and Isobel was only wearing a light dress.

"I think you need your pelisse. Have you chosen the woods as our venue?"

"No, and don't worry. It's not far." She pointed at the external greenhouse.

Of course, he should have realized. They had never used it, but he'd been assured by his agent that it was in good working order. Since the conservatory had been more convenient for their use, he'd never even bothered to go inside. As far as he knew no one else did either. Isobel had chosen well.

The inside of the greenhouse was a large rectangular space. Old work benches and tables lined the walls, leaving a cleared area in the center. Grooves in the dirt showed that Isobel must have recently moved the tables herself. Other miscellaneous garden tools and supplies were stacked in the corner nearest the door.

The cleared space wasn't empty. A large circle, bisected in half, had been drawn in white in the dirt. It was surrounded by a few crates filled with small boxes and little bottles. A larger dark brown glass bottle stoppered with cork and wax was set in front of the boxes. On the other side of the circle rested a small stack of kindling. There was an unlit lantern next to it.

"You've been busy. I'm sorry you had to do all of this on your own," he observed.

"It wasn't all that much work," she said dismissively, but the tension in her posture was obvious.

Now that they were in the greenhouse she was moving stiffly, the line of her shoulders unnaturally straight. He wanted to reassure her, but his own anxiety was eating at him.

Watching with interest, his eyes tracked her as she reached into the crate for a small box and began pouring more white powder on the circle's diameter. It glittered oddly.

"I thought that was chalk, but it's something else isn't it? Some sort of mineral? Powdered quartz or some other semi-precious stone?"

Isobel smiled as she lit the lamp, the light casting a golden glow on her face. She had never looked more beautiful. But then again, he thought that every time he saw her.

"It's salt, actually."

That wasn't what he'd been expecting. "Salt?"

"A substance of vastly underestimated properties."

He snorted slightly. "A bit like governesses."

Her eyes glowed in the lamplight, but she didn't reply. "You should take off your shirt for this. I think direct contact with your skin will help," she said with a duck of her head and a trace of apology in her voice.

Feeling a bit more like his old self, he gave her a teasing smile.

"If you wanted to see my bare chest, there's no need to make excuses," he said as he pulled off his waistcoat and thick cotton shirt. "All you ever need to do is ask."

She didn't smile back. "Unfortunately, direct contact with your skin means a greater likelihood of sustaining burns. In this case, they would be to your chest, just here," she said, placing her hand high on her stomach.

"Why there? Wouldn't over my head be a more likely choice?"

Isobel fiddled with a piece of kindling. "I've no wish to burn your face off, my lord. I've grown quite fond of it. And the choice is signifi-cant. It's something my grandmother taught me that I've been able to confirm with my reading. There are centers of power in the body, sort of like openings. A trained practitioner can access some of these with their healing if they're skilled enough or..."

"Or open a gateway to curse someone," he said heavily.

She nodded. "Their number varies depending on the culture of the person writing the account. On average there are seven. I had initially thought to choose the one just below," she said, moving her hand down her stomach with a tightening of her cheeks. "It's the one usually associated with sexual release, but after doing more reading, I decided the one above it would suit us better."

She turned away hastily to organize a few things around the circle, a series of flat white stones. Once they were in position, she grabbed another box with a fine grey powder and drew lines between the stones.

"Are you sure? The one associated with...being amorous certainly sounds like a fine candidate," he said awkwardly.

Turning back toward him, she nodded quickly. "I thought so too at first, but the one above is tied to your personal will, and yours has been overpowered by this other being. I believe it will serve us better. Besides, we don't want to damage you...lower. I'm still hoping to have a family someday."

The last was said in a lighthearted tone, but it made his throat tighten. "I'd like that, too."

It was hard to stifle the rush of warm optimism that was running through him now. His wife was a brilliant woman, who possessed a great deal of raw talent and power. If anyone could get him through this, it was her. And he would spend the rest of his life thanking her for it.

"You sit here, but don't disturb the salt. We can't break the circle," she instructed, gesturing to it with a sweep of her hand.

Sucking in a deep breath, he stepped carefully over the line of salt and lowered himself into a seated position. Isobel did the same, taking extra care with her skirts. She reached for the brown bottle.

"You have to drink this." She handed him the bottle, her face pale. "Don't do so until I say, and then brace yourself because it will cause a lot of pain. You must take care to bear it as best you can. The circle must not be disturbed, so you mustn't move, at least not overmuch."

He nodded and took the brown bottle.

"Not yet," she admonished with a finger before reaching out for a large piece of wood from the kindling.

Next she placed her hand on the lantern and closed her eyes. It sounded like she was whispering, soft words he couldn't make out but sounded vaguely like Latin. With a spill of bright sparks, the length of wood began to smoke and then flared into a blazing orange flame.

He swore. It was the damnedest thing he'd ever seen. Peeking from behind her lashes, Isobel squinted at the torch before relaxing and smiling at him.

"I've been practicing," she said with a nod at the flame. "It won't go out until it's over. It's charmed."

"Impressive, *bella mia*," he said, slightly out of breath.

"Don't compliment me yet." She sighed, almost vibrating with tension.

"It's going to be all right, *mi amore*."

"I'm supposed to be telling you that."

Time seemed to stand still for a moment. She gave him another anxious glance, then nodded at the bottle.

He looked down at it, breaking the seal of the wax stopper with a twist. The smell of the liquid inside was overpowering, a strange mixture of metal, earth, and cloves. Coughing slightly, he raised the bottle in a toast before downing the contents in a quick pull.

For a long moment nothing happened. He parted his lips to ask Isobel if something had gone wrong. The blinding wave of pain took him by surprise. It rolled through his abdomen, burning like acid as it went. In seconds the pain radiated to his extremities.

It was as if he was already on fire. Every single part of his body was crying out. He could feel a fierce shaking and knew he was having convulsions. Opening his eyes with effort, he checked the line of salt around him to make sure he hadn't broken the barrier.

He'd managed—only just—to stay in his half of the circle. Catching a glimpse of his love through watery eyes, he saw her face was deathly white.

"Matteo, I'm going to begin now. Please try to hold on!"

She was barely beginning *now*?

Marshaling all his strength, he nodded, his neck rigid. The movement was a mistake. It was as if his head was going to snap off. He didn't attempt it again, focusing his concentration was on staying as still as possible. Then his beautiful wife made everything a thousand times worse.

Heat. Excruciating. Unbearable. All of it was focused on his torso, the space directly above his stomach. He looked down, expecting to see a mass of blistering burning flesh—or a gaping hole—where his chest used to be. But his skin was intact. Terribly red, but otherwise normal.

Isobel was holding the torch against his middle, but the flame wasn't touching him. And it *should* have been.

There was a hairsbreadth of space between him at the fire. But the flame was kept from direct contact with his skin by an invisible wall. It shaped the fire into a near perfect circle. As he trembled and jerked closer to her, the unseen barrier adjusted, following his movements.

There was something else too. A crawling sensation in his veins, like mercury running through them. It circled through his body like a rat trying to escape a flood.

It was the demon.

Aware of soft murmuring, he squinted at Isobel. She was saying something, more Latin words. He didn't try to understand what they were. Squeezing his eyes shut, he gritted his teeth, trying not to crush them with the force he was exerting, trying to keep his body from flying apart.

Through all the chaos, a new sensation became apparent. It was as if something was pulling at his core, drawing on him like a sucking leech.

And then all hell broke loose.

CHAPTER 27

"What the hell is this?" Aldo Garibaldi roared.

Isobel's head flew up, her concentration breaking. The fire made contact with Matteo's skin. His skin blistered and the hair on his chest begin to burn. Pulling the torch back, she turned to the *Conte*.

"No! Stay where you are!" she yelled, fighting the urge to jump up to slap him. "You'll ruin everything."

The *Conte* walked closer to the circle. "What are you doing?"

"What you wanted me to do," she hissed. "Stay there. Don't move and be quiet!"

Aldo's face contorted at the sight of Matteo, who'd crumpled over on his side. "You will release my son. You're killing him!"

Bloody stupid idiot.

"I'm trying to save him," she said in shocked disbelief as the *Conte* raged at her. "And don't you dare breach this circle!" She scrambled to her knees to grab a second piece of kindling, brandishing it in the count's direction.

"I know you're trying to kill him. Nino told me everything."

What fresh hell was this? "He was *wrong*. Now shut up and stay away."

"Don't tell—"

"Father, stay away."

Isobel gasped, turning back to her husband. Matteo's voice was low and raspy, strained beyond all reason. She didn't know how he had managed to speak. His body was being wracked by deep bone-shaking tremors and his face was nearly purple.

Tears running freely down her cheeks, she reached out to touch him again.

"Matteo my love, please hold on," she cried, sitting back down. "We can still do this. Don't move!"

"No, you *can't!*"

Dizzily, Isobel twisted her head to the door. The last had been yelled by someone else. Another man had intruded on her ritual. He had to step closer to the lantern light for her to recognize him. And the gun he was holding.

"Nino, what the bloody hell is going on?" the *Conte* yelled. "You said she was going to kill my son, that she was planning on running away with all of his money. *My* money."

Nino advanced, completely ignoring the count. The gun was pointed directly at her. "You weren't supposed to get this far. You weren't supposed to be here at all," he said hoarsely.

"Please let me finish, Nino. I can save him," she pleaded.

He leaned forward, his face contorting in anger. "I know that, but you're not going to. You're going to let him die."

Isobel's heart sank.

"What the hell are you saying?" the *Conte* asked in a strangled voice.

The true horror of it all was finally becoming clear. "He's saying he did this," she whispered. "He's responsible for the curse."

It was a guess, but one Nino didn't contradict. He approached the circle instead, frowning down at it.

Isobel gasped. "Don't even think it!"

He narrowed his eyes at her. "I won't break the circle. I know the demon will escape then. No other innocent will be harmed. There's been enough death already. But you're not going to finish. Stand, right now, and walk away. You can escape. No one will blame you." He swung the gun at the *Conte* and Matteo respectively. "These two will stay here and die."

A small move from Aldo distracted Nino, who swung the rifle at him in response.

"I don't understand," Aldo said, bewildered. "Why are you doing this? You've been a loyal servant throughout this whole ordeal."

Nino laughed. "I've been a loyal servant far longer than that actually." His face was lit with an unwholesome excitement, as if he'd been waiting for this confrontation. "And you didn't even recognize me, the senior game warden from your Tivoli country estate. But why would you? You prefer indoor pursuits, don't you?"

"What the hell does that mean?" Aldo said.

Hefting the gun higher, Nino threw him a look full of hatred. "It means I know what you did to my daughter, you bastard! You and your friends."

"What daughter? I don't know what you're talking about!"

Nino gave a choking laugh. "The sad part is that I believe you. You've ruined and murdered so many girls over the years. Why would my Gina stand out in your memory?"

"I've never killed anyone, let alone a woman!"

"Then where is she, *figlio di cane?*"

The *Conte* shrugged helplessly. "I don't know! I have no idea who you're talking about."

Shaking with rage, Nino raised the gun again, his finger beginning to squeeze the trigger.

"Stop!" Isobel yelled. "At least tell him when your daughter disappeared. And what she looked like! Maybe he'll remember."

Nino paused, turning to look at her. "It was three summers ago. She was a beautiful girl with rosy cheeks and light golden brown hair. Gina favored her mother."

Behind him, the count's expression changed. He did remember the girl. But the guilt on his face told her knowing the full story would only make things worse.

"Nino, please explain something to me," she said. "If you think the

Conte is responsible, why are you punishing Matteo? Or do you think he harmed your Gina as well?"

"Matteo wasn't even home that summer," the *Conte* interjected. "He was traveling the continent with his friends."

Nino said nothing.

"Is that true, Nino? If it is, why are you doing this?" She gestured at her fallen husband who was still writhing and panting for air in quick tortured breaths.

"He took my only child...so I'm going to take his."

"But why this way? This curse, the way he was before I met him— all of those deaths. There were so many innocents lost. He couldn't stop. Why harm so many others, vulnerable women just like your daughter?"

A flash of pain passed over Nino's face. "What did I care after my Gina was gone?" he cried.

Isobel stilled. He was lying.

"There weren't supposed to be any innocents, were there? The first demon didn't kill indiscriminately, did it? It was supposed to kill Aldo and any of his peers."

"I don't understand," Aldo rasped.

She swung around to face him. "Matteo's first bad spell happened unexpectedly. You said you were going to have a gathering that weekend—a party. And the first victim was one of your friends."

Mouth dropping open, Aldo nodded and Nino made a choking sound.

"I should have known better than to ask for what I did," Nino said. "It was stupid of me not to realize that the *Conte* would gladly sacrifice those beneath him to feed the demon's bloodlust. The best I could do was seek employment as one of Matteo's minders and wait till he self-destructed. At least the *Conte* would have to watch his paragon of a son, his pride and joy, deteriorate into madness. It was only a matter of time. I knew how the curse worked, what the signs of the demon's emergence would be."

It made a twisted sort of sense, and she found herself acknowledging his story with a nod.

"And so it was safe enough for you to be near Matteo, watching and waiting to make sure your plan succeeded. But you didn't cast the curse did you? You said you asked for it..."

Nino acknowledged her words with a tilt of his head. "It took every cent I had, and months of waiting for the witch to do the work. He came all the way from Sicily, but it was worth it. In the end, he even gave me a discount. Aldo Garibaldi has destroyed many lives with his rapacious business practices, overcharging tenants and pushing people off their land. It was only a matter of time to find a connection the witch would care about. He was happy to help. I never expected the *Conte* would find another with enough skill and power to undo it all."

Isobel cast a helpless glance at her husband. He was trembling violently now, and the hole in his aura she'd made had expanded into a gaping wound. Nothing else could invade since he'd fallen in the circle of salt, but he couldn't survive like that for long. She needed to finish and close the hole.

She drew Nino's attention back to her. "You wanted me to run away."

His first words to her had been about Ottavio falling asleep during his watch and he'd paid close attention to everything she did in the conservatory. He'd probably spied on her notes in the library as well, else he wouldn't have known that she had finished formulating her purge ritual.

Or that you were brewing a tea to prevent pregnancy. Ottavio must have learned that detail from Nino.

Nino's eye twitched. "I'm sorry you got involved in all of this. That wasn't supposed to happen. I thought it was just a fluke that you survived, but then it became obvious what you were. You survived because of your power. Then the demon changed. In time it would kill the son, but you delayed that. And then it looked like you were finally figuring out how to remove the curse," he said, gesturing to the ritual circle. "Which is why I sent Ottavio to you."

It felt like the room was spinning. Isobel felt sick. "You had him attack me?" she whispered.

162

Nino squeezed his eyes shut, shaking his head. "That wasn't supposed to happen, either! You were supposed to run away with him. Women always liked him, and he wanted you. I thought you would jump at the opportunity to escape. But you were so stupid—another fool woman. You'd already given your heart to the monster," he spat, lowering the barrel slightly as he sneered at her.

It was the opportunity she'd been waiting for. She flew up from her kneeling position, holding the burning torch with a death grip. She swung it a Nino as hard as she could.

The blow struck him in the shoulder, making him drop the gun.

She should have expected what happened next. The fire was no normal blaze...and she was very angry. As soon as it came in contact with Nino's clothing it exploded, running over him like a wild creature. His shriek of pain was enough to shatter glass. He fell to his knees, clutching blindly.

Isobel scrambled forward, crawling toward him. She had to try and control the fire enough to pull it away from him. But she didn't get the chance. Nino pulled a blade from his boot and sprang up with a blood-curdling scream.

He was almost on her when he was thrown to the side. The *Conte* was pushing him with his forearms, kicking him hard. Nino landed face down, wheezing with a horribly wet sound. Using his booted foot, Aldo turned him over.

The blade was sticking out of his chest. He had landed on it when he fell. Aldo leaned over him, obscuring him from view.

"Matteo," she whispered, dragging herself to her feet. Twisting, she reached for the fallen torch, but it wasn't there.

She turned back to the circle, dismayed to find she'd disturbed her half's salt boundary. But that wasn't the worst thing that met her sight.

Matteo's long arms had been enough to reach the torch. He was holding it to his chest exactly where she had, his whole body wrapped around it.

"No! Matteo, let go," she said, falling to her feet in front of him.

Using all her strength, she tried to pry it out of his hands but he had a death grip on it.

"It's too late," he whispered. "Going to finish it now." He turned to cradle the fire underneath him—out of her reach.

"No, no. Don't do this. Please give me the torch," she cried tearfully, stepping into his half of the circle and throwing herself on his back. She embraced him from behind and begged with a sob. "Please don't leave me."

He shuddered and didn't answer as he tried to push her away. Isobel held on tighter, wrapped around his back like a limpet. Looking inside him with her other sight, she pushed down with all strength, finding the taint and directing it to the hole in his solar plexus.

The demon scrabbled inside him, tearing at Matteo's aura as it tried to hang on. Using all of her will and every ounce of her strength, she kept going until it lost its grip and was forced down into the fire burning underneath her husband.

A rending sound filled the air. The count shifted looking around wildly for its source, but what had made the noise wasn't visible. The painful clatter died away and Isobel's ears popped, as if the air had shifted dramatically around them.

"Let go, my darling. It's over. I swear it's over. Please!" she said, rolling her husband onto his back and throwing the burning wood away.

Nausea rose up when she saw his hands and abdomen. They were a raw mass of blistered meat, black and red. The smell of cooked flesh filled the air.

Sobbing, she gathered Matteo's large body to her as best she could, cradling him in her lap. Closing her eyes, she began to chant, trying to bind the ragged edges of his aura back together. But it had been ripped and exposed so long, it had splintered and cracked in other places. Trying to force the edges closed tore open others.

Isobel refused to let go. She covered him with her body and her mind, instinctively trying to hold him together. Giving everything she had, she clung to him, past reason and all endurance.

The world around them spun into black. She fell into the void, still holding on.

CHAPTER 28

*I*sobel cracked open an eyelid in the bright sunny bedroom. Everything hurt. She felt like she'd been passed through a meat grinder. Her aura probably had been.

A noise made her turn. It was Aldo, shifting impatiently in a chair.

When he saw she was awake, he nodded at her. "It's over now. I told him the truth before he died."

Isobel burst into tears. "Matteo's *dead?*"

Aldo flinched and gave her an apologetic glance. "No. He's...sleeping. I meant Nino. About his daughter."

She sat up and crossed her arms. "You do remember her."

It was a statement of fact.

The *Conte* nodded. "And she is dead, but I never harmed her. Gina died in childbirth."

Understanding dawned. "And the babe was yours."

"Yes. I never let any of my friends share her. She didn't want that and I respected her choice. And I didn't force her either. I made sure Nino knew that. And about the child."

Surprised, she narrowed her eyes. "The child lived?"

Aldo inhaled, drawing himself up. "Yes. It's being taken care of."

Out of sight and out of mind, she thought. *What a mess.*

"Does Matteo know?"

He looked away. "He has enough to worry about."

That was more than enough to get her out of bed. She stood up stiffly. "Where is he?"

He gestured to the connecting door, and she hurried through it to Matteo's bedroom.

Her chest squeezed her heart when she saw him. His aura was intact—mostly. A few glints of green, the distinctive shade of her own aura, could be seen here and there. She picked up her hand and examined the shimmering haze surrounding it. A few prominent streaks of red ran through it.

Somehow she'd blended their auras, weaving hers over the tears in his. In turn, some of his had been transferred to her.

We'll always be tied together now.

Unfortunately, Matteo's hands and chest hadn't fared as well. They were wrapped in white gauze, but badly. Bits of burned flesh were visible between the strips. And it was starting to seep. If she didn't clean the flesh and change the bandages, it would grow infected.

"I didn't really know what to do and neither did the staff," Aldo murmured "We sent for a physician, but the sawbones was soused and could barely stand. I didn't let him near my son. I was going to send for another doctor, but I think you can do better."

Isobel walked up to her husband, inspecting him closely. She nodded in agreement. "Go fetch me clean gauze and scissors. I'll need the crates in the greenhouse, as well. The one's holding all of my supplies."

"Will he live?"

Leaning over, she put her hand on Matteo's chest. His breathing was shallow, but even, and his heart was steady. His aura looked bad, but it would mend.

"Yes, I think so," she whispered.

"What about his hands?"

She glanced down at them. They were curled into claws, likely a reflex to all of the damage. Whether or not he would be able to use them again was doubtful.

"I don't know, but we can't go waste any more time. My things, please," she said, waving him away.

Once he was gone, she sat on the bed. To her relief, Matteo's lids fluttered and opened. Despite the pain he must be suffering from, he smiled weakly at her.

"Still alive, *bella,* and all alone."

Isobel frowned, and was about to assure him she wasn't going to leave him when what he meant became clear. There was no "other" in his body anymore, and he could feel it.

Inhaling deeply, she relaxed. Pressing a kiss to his forehead, she whispered, "Yes, my love, you are."

CHAPTER 29

*D*ays passed in anxious vigil. Isobel tended to Matteo's burns with healing poultices and restorative draughts, getting little sleep. What rest she did get was snatched sitting up in bed at his side.

But day-by-day he improved and eventually the risk of infection passed. The burn on his chest scabbed over and by moving gingerly he was able to sit up and eventually stand and walk.

Unfortunately, his hands were far worse off. The skin had been badly burned and the musculature deeply damaged. He couldn't move them. They hung at his sides, lifeless claws he couldn't open or close. Without a miracle, it was likely he would never be able to use them again.

Despite being witness and catalyst to the events in the greenhouse, the count couldn't stop from criticizing her role. Upset over Matteo's hands, he cornered her in the parlor a few days later. He argued that she should have found a way that wouldn't have left his son scarred if things went wrong.

Hanging onto her temper by a thread she defended herself, and Matteo, who had been willing to risk everything—including death—than live with that blackness in his soul.

"And let's not forget exactly why we are here now," she added through gritted teeth. "This is because of you and your arrogance and sense of self-entitlement."

"What does that mean?" he argued back.

"*Gina*."

He scoffed. "I provided for the child and would have done so for the mother had she lived."

In spite of everything that had happened, all the damage and destruction he had witnessed, his tone was still dismissive. Nino's revenge hadn't been enough to pierce his thick shell of overblown sense of privilege. She was about to blister his ears when they were interrupted.

"You may have provided for your other child, but have you acknowledged him? Or is it a her?"

Matteo was standing in the doorway of the parlor. He was dressed in the same breeches she'd helped him into that morning. He'd somehow managed to throw a shirt over his shoulders, but left it hanging open over his bandaged chest.

"Son, you're awake," Aldo said, twisting to face the door.

Matteo nodded slowly and then turned to smile weakly at Isobel before looking back to his father. "And you still haven't said whether or not I have a brother or a sister."

Aldo frowned. "That doesn't matter. I've already told you, the child is provided for."

Matteo came inside and sat next to Isobel on the settee. "And what kind of life do they have?"

His father's mouth firmed. "A perfectly decent one. One of my tenant farmers took the babe. He and his wife had no children at the time. It was a good fit for him."

"Him?" Matteo narrowed his eyes at his father. "My brother is going to be a tenant farmer? On an estate I will someday inherit?"

His mouth twisted in distaste.

The count tsked. "He's a *bastard*. I've made arrangements for him. He'll get his own plot someday," he said with the air of someone who felt truly magnanimous.

169

"That's not good enough. He should get his fair share."

"He is getting what he deserves. Few illegitimate children are so lucky."

"And whose fault is it that the boy isn't legitimate?" Matteo said, forgetting himself and throwing up his bandaged hands before wincing.

Aldo swore. "What did you expect me to do? Marry his mother?"

"Why not?" Matteo yelled.

The *Conte* looked at him as if he'd lost his mind. "You *don't* marry a domestic," he said incredulously.

"I did," he replied quietly.

Isobel turned to Matteo, slipping her hand behind his back to rub it in small circles.

Aldo passed a hand over his face "A governess is different. Her father was a gentleman."

She suppressed an ironic smile.

"Well, at least you acknowledge that much," Matteo said quietly.

Rubbing his face with both hands, Aldo sighed loudly. "We can discuss this later. You need your rest. I'm going to go home."

Matteo leaned forward. "I think that's a good idea."

Sighing, Aldo rose. "I'll call again tomorrow."

"No. I think it would be a good idea if you went home to Italy."

His father stared at him, hurt deepening the grooves on either side of his mouth.

"It's for the best, father," Matteo continued.

"But you're still injured..."

Matteo glanced at Isobel. "I'll be in good hands. In fact, I'll probably heal much better if we're on our own," he added gently. "Once I'm able to travel we'll follow."

His father frowned. "When?" he asked.

"Soon," Matteo sighed, giving her a sideways glance. "The climate of this country doesn't suit me."

Inhaling deeply, Aldo finally nodded. "All right, but you'll come directly home once you're able?"

"We will see," Matteo said slowly.

They said their goodbyes, but Matteo stopped Aldo at the doorway.

"Father, we're not done talking about my brother yet," he added.

Aldo sighed loudly, his shoulders slumping before he nodded.

Once he was gone, there was silence. Matteo just stood there, looking at the doorway for several moments.

Isobel marched up to him. "Bed. *Now*."

He smiled slightly. "Yes, madame witch. Your wish is my command."

UPSTAIRS, Isobel changed Matteo's bandages with quick efficiency. He was quiet, his face grave throughout the procedure. When she tried to give him a healing tonic, one she hoped would help repair the musculature of his hands, he shook his head.

"Darling, what's wrong?"

Matteo cocked his head at her, giving her a wry glance. He gestured down at himself with a quick motion of his head.

She sighed. "The scarring will improve. In time, you'll be able to walk normally. My grandmother's poultices will help keep the skin soft and pliant enough to stretch. This tonic will help the damaged muscles. There's every chance you may regain some use in your hands. You mustn't give up hope."

He closed his eyes and shook his head. "No. No more tonics. I don't deserve hope...or to get better."

Isobel kneeled in front of him. "Of course you do. It's normal to grow despondent when you're facing a long recovery."

"This isn't melancholia. This," he held up his hands, "is penance. I did so many horrible things, in reality I deserve so much worse. And you...you deserve only the best. Your freedom—and a man to love who isn't tainted. Someone who's not disfigured. That's one of the reasons I asked my father to go on ahead. As soon as he departs for Italy, you can leave."

Hurt, Isobel glared at him with tears in her eyes.

"It's all right, *mi amore*," he assured her earnestly. "I'll buy you a house anywhere you want and make sure you have everything you need. Your own accounts. With all you've done for me, you deserve your freedom."

"Do you honestly believe that after everything we've been through I'm going to leave you *now*? Are you insane?"

His mouth opened and closed a few times. "Isabella, I'm a murderer."

"*No*, Nino is, as well as the witch who cursed you. And if there is more blood on someone else's hands then it's your father who deserves his share—not you. More than his share! And you forget I heard all of Nino's story. He admitted you were innocent of any wrongdoing. The curse was meant to punish your father. What they did to you was a crime. You were the victim, and now that I've gone through the trouble of saving you I will not be cheated."

"Cheated?"

Isobel stood up and put her hands on her hips. "Yes, *cheated*. Did you or did you not promise that if I saved you, you would spend the rest of your life loving and cherishing me? Because I recall that you did—several times. So don't try to tell me now that you were wrong or you made a mistake!"

Tears welled in his eyes. "There was no mistake. I've loved you since the moment I saw you. Even though my mind wasn't always my own, my heart recognized you. But you deserve better than this," he said, lifting his hands in emphasis.

"What I deserve is your love and devotion, all of the happiness you promised. And I will get it because, damn it, I earned it!"

Matteo's eyes grew bright with unspent tears, but he burst out laughing. "Yes, you did, and then some. If you are really willing to settle for an over-privileged and self-entitled *conticino,* then I'll do my best to fulfill all of my promises."

Relaxing, Isobel sighed and sat down next to him on the bed. "I don't think those words have ever applied to you. You are nothing like your father. And I'll expect more than your best," she said with a playful nudge.

Eyes remote, he nodded. "Anything you want. And I'm not insulted. Truthfully, I've been thinking that my father and I need some...distance. Perhaps a lot of distance."

"I know. You told him to go ahead to Italy."

He swallowed. "I meant after we travel home. I have another small estate on the Lago di Bolsena. I inherited it from my grandmother. She used to make it her home when she was the dowager countess. Father doesn't like it much because it's not as grand as our other estates, but my mother loved it and I do too. I think that's where we should make our home. If Father wants to see us, he can do so there. But only to visit. We should live on our own."

Isobel put her hands over her heart, shoulders shaking in relief. "We don't have to live with your father? Oh, thank the stars. That's the best news I've ever heard."

Matteo laughed again before wincing and subsided.

"Lean back, darling," she urged, gently pushing at his shoulders to recline him on the pillows of his bed.

Unfastening his breeches, she tugged them down.

"Isabella, I've had enough sleep to last me a lifetime. There's no way I'm going to bed right now."

Laughing to herself, she pulled the cloth free of his legs. "Actually, I had something else in mind," she said, beginning to unfasten her dress.

His eyes lit up. "And what might that be?" he asked, even as it became increasingly obvious that she was wiggling out of her gown.

"Well," she began, joining him on the bed. "It occurs to me that this is the first time we've been alone together. Truly alone."

He coughed, his hips rising as she reached out to massage his legs and then higher.

"I suppose that's one way of looking at it." His expression grew serious. "But what if..."

"If what?"

He glanced at her and then away quickly. "Suppose you like it better the other way? I still remember how intense it was. I don't want to disappoint you now that I'm just a man," he said in a low hoarse voice.

Her brow rose pointedly. "You could never do that."

He looked at his hands and grimaced. "I can't even touch you."

"Yes, you can." She smiled softly before pulling off her chemise and crawling to his side. "Everywhere," she whispered as she offered him her breasts.

He hesitated before latching onto the creamy mounds eagerly, kissing and sucking each in turn. Shifting closer to her, he drew the rapidly hardening tip of one into his mouth and laved it, and then the other, with his tongue. Isobel moaned, parting her legs involuntarily.

It did feel different this time, more intense.

Her husband must have thought so too. "*Cara*, use your hand. Touch yourself for me," he rasped. "Open your legs wider so I can see."

Blushing hotly, she complied. Moving over, she positioned herself closer to his head, parting her legs.

His eyes caressed her, so hot she could feel herself growing moist from his gaze alone. Tentatively she touched between her legs, running her fingers up and down over her tender inner lips. She teased herself under his watchful dark eyes, playing with the little nub above her sex until she was breathing heavily.

So was he. "Isabella, climb over me—over my face. I want to taste you."

A thrill passed through her at the idea. He moved down to lie flat on the bed. Heart racing, she shifted and threw her leg over him, positioning herself on her knees just over his face. Using the headboard to brace herself, she lowered those crucial few inches until he was there, pressing an open-mouthed kiss to her soft feminine flesh.

That caress reverberated through her body. Hands trembling, Isobel gripped the headboard tighter.

"You taste like nothing else, *mi amore*," he whispered, his hot breath puffing over her wet sex. "Move yourself as you will. I want you to guide me."

Isobel looked down, meeting his eyes. It was so strange to see him smiling up at her from between her legs. She laughed and nodded, adjusting her hips so that she was hovering above him, shifting up and down so that his lips and tongue could caress her.

"Oh, God," she gasped as he sucked her pearl into his mouth. Above him she writhed, rocking back and forth as his mouth worked its magic underneath her.

His tongue probed her entrance, forcing its way inside her in a wicked twisting motion. The spasms started almost immediately. Her channel gripped him like a velvet vise, throbbing around him. Losing control, Isobel threw her head back and rocked faster until she was grinding down on him.

Her scream of completion made him laugh, but it was muffled and Isobel hastily collapsed to the side so she wouldn't smother him.

It took several minutes to catch her breath. When she finally turned to look at him, he was watching her breasts heave up and down with each movement of her chest.

"It's hell not being able to touch you, *cara*," he said, twin notes of longing and frustration in his voice.

Poor Matteo, he truly did not deserve to lose the use of his hands.

"I would like to remind you, my lord, that the night isn't over yet."

He chuckled and she shifted down the bed, moving over him until her head was level with his manhood.

Tentatively, she reached out to lick him.

"What are you doing, *amore?*" he asked breathlessly.

"Something the maids used to whisper about...the things they did when they went out walking with their sweetheart. It was considered safe since they didn't risk their positions by falling pregnant."

Taking his already swollen manhood in her hands, she put her mouth over the rounded head, licking and sucking, cupping him below and squeezing lightly. Experimenting, she tried to take as much of him in her mouth as she could, but he was too big, so she settled for kissing him up and down his length.

Matteo didn't seem to care that she couldn't take all of him. His moans filled the air. She liked the sound and the fact that *she* was the one causing it. It was his turn to writhe helplessly, to be taken to the brink and then pushed over it.

His hips thrust up, trying to prolong the contact with the warmth of her mouth until he suddenly changed his mind.

"*Cara*, stop. Please. I need to be inside you."

Still riding the high from pleasuring him she climbed over his thighs, bringing them together with a heady rush of sensual abandon.

The air in her lungs escaped in a hiss as she sank down on his steely arousal. He was almost too large and thick for her—especially in this position—but she was soft and hot from her earlier climax, enough to work his entire length inside.

He swore when the tip of him touched her womb, but quickly lost the power of speech when she began to move. Leaning forward and using her arms for leverage, she rose up until he was about to slip out and then quickly back down.

Below her, he reached up reflexively. His bandaged hands pressed against her hips.

She hurriedly leaned down to whisper, "No, my darling. You mustn't."

He needed to be careful. Taking hold of his wrists, she pressed his arms down to the bed, holding him by the forearms so he couldn't hurt himself.

She pressed a kiss to his lips before beginning to rock again. Clasping him tightly in her sheath, she pumped up and down, losing herself in the feel of him. Her sheath gripped his shaft hungrily, the friction she generated catalyzing pleasure to blinding ecstasy.

Giving herself over to the moment, she cried out, hips rocking frantically as her climax rose and crested like a wave. It crashed down with the force of the ocean during a storm.

Inside of her, Matteo's cock swelled and pulsed as his shout mingled with her own. Holding herself tight around him as the last tremors rocked their bodies, she just barely stopped herself from falling forward onto his bandaged chest.

The words he was chanting finally penetrated her bliss-fogged mind. "*Ti amo, sempre.*"

"Too overcome to speak, she concentrated on regaining the will to move. After a long minute she slipped to the left, pushing up against his side until her breasts and sex were pressed against his arm and hip.

"I love you, too," she finally whispered back, stopping his chant with a touch of her fingers.

He kissed the tips briefly before speaking again.

"Thank you," he breathed.

"For what? I mean aside from the obvious..." she asked with a teasing smile, turning to look up at him.

"For everything. For saving me and for staying," he said, the love in his eyes warming her down to her soul.

She reached up to touch his cheek. "You forgot something."

"What?" He frowned.

"To thank me for proving that what we have now—just the two of us—is better than anything that came before."

His eyes lingered on her face with a loving expression. "I know that's true for me. I'm just grateful you feel the same way. And know this, as soon as I can hold you in my arms again, I'm never letting go."

"Good," she murmured, pressing her brow against his shoulder.

Because she didn't plan on letting go either. And because he had just given her a brilliant idea...

EPILOGUE

FIVE MONTHS LATER.

"And this is mint," Isobel said in a much-improved Italian accent, pointing to the dark green leaves. "In addition to its pleasing taste, it is very beneficial for the digestion as well as other minor ailments."

Little Tomas leaned over to inspect the plant she was holding, his small brow creased in concentration. He didn't reply, but that wasn't unusual. He was incredibly intelligent, but Tomas was still growing accustomed to her presence. The only person he was truly comfortable with was his older brother Matteo, whom he called Papa.

Though shy with her, Tomas did like plants. He would silently trail her in the greenhouse Matteo had built for her whenever she was working in there. That had given her the idea to teach him about herbology.

In addition to the greenhouse, their countryside home had extensive gardens as well as several small streams and a fantastic view of the crystalline waters of lake Bolsena.

She made good use of the fertile land, growing everything she needed for her healing practice. There was a lot to teach Tomas about plants and the natural world. She even let him observe when the local villagers came to her for cures to their minor complaints. And despite his tender years, he paid close attention to everything she taught him.

It had been Isobel's idea to claim Tomas as her son from a previous marriage. No one in Italy knew her, she reasoned, so there was little chance their lie would be discovered. They spread the story after Thomas' adopted parents agreed to give him up.

The family that had taken him in had just found out they were expecting a second babe. After visiting them, Matteo had become convinced that Tomas was already being neglected in favor of their own son. The problem would only grow worse with a new child, so he'd given them a substantial financial gift and claimed his brother as his own—but not before warning her that no one would believe he was hers. The boy was too obviously a Garibaldi. Everyone would assume he'd sired a bastard before they met.

Isobel didn't give a fig about the gossip. Despite his reticence with her, she adored Tomas. He was so much like Matteo, it was impossible not to love him. Though unnaturally reserved, the little boy was bright and considerate.

I can only hope to be as lucky with our own child, she thought pensively chewing her lip.

Forcing her attention back to Tomas, she continued her lesson. Today that included letting him plant his own strawberry seeds. They would grow year round in the greenhouse.

Once the *Conte* had discovered they'd taken his bastard in, he stopped visiting them in the country—although he still demanded Matteo visit him on occasion at their estate in Santa Fiora. Her husband obliged, mainly because Nino's plot had brought his father's business practices to his attention. He wanted to make sure the tenants and staff on all their estates were being treated well.

Isobel never went with him. Her feelings for the *Conte* were complicated and she couldn't seem to keep from fighting with him.

Matteo didn't mind visiting without her. He wanted time alone with his father so he could pressure him into revealing the where-abouts of his other bastards. From what Nino had said, there had to be more of them. Matteo had been wary about claiming them all, arguing that it wasn't fair to her, but Isobel insisted she wanted a big family.

However, the *Conte* was adamant he had no other children, so for the time being there was only Tomas. And soon their own child.

Another pang of disquiet passed through her. Don't assume the worst, she lectured herself sternly as she contemplated her swollen middle.

Thankfully she was distracted when Tomas' nurse came to collect him. It was time for his luncheon and then nap. Isobel said goodbye and was intensely gratified when the little one consented to be kissed. She was definitely winning him over.

Planting the rest of the strawberry seeds on her own, she placed the finished pots on a sunny table. Sprinkling some of her grand-mother's special growing solution in each pot, she said a little chant for their speedy growth. It was another recipe she'd found in Helen's books, one she found extremely useful. Especially since both Tomas and Matteo seemed overly fond of hothouse strawberries.

"I knew I'd find you in here."

Isobel turned to see her husband coming through the greenhouse doors. He was looking very fine, in a loose linen shirt and breeches. Despite the heat of the day, he was wearing black kidskin gloves over his hands. Watching him approach, she flushed at the memory of those black gloves moving all over her nude body the night before.

Though he still bore scars, the underlying musculature of his hands had improved markedly. He could use them with only a little pain now—despite his continued refusal to let her apply more salves, or to drink any of the tonics she prepared for him. Even after they moved to Italy, he insisted the injuries were his penance.

As a witness and first-hand participant in those dark events, she understood. As his wife, she refused to let him continue to punish himself for something that had been out of his control.

However, in recent days, Matteo had become skeptical. His hands had recovered too quickly and too well for him not to suspect her. She'd heard him asking his valet if she'd given the cook anything to add to his food or drink. His lack of trust wounded her a little, but since she *was* healing him on the sly she decided not to dwell on it.

At least the suspicious glint in his eye didn't stop him from gathering her into his arms and kissing her soundly in greeting. Softening in his embrace, she returned his kiss eagerly. His gloved hands cupped the back of her head before moving down to stretch over her swollen belly.

"How is she today?"

"Active. And it's a he," she said pointedly.

She knew it for a fact.

Matteo raised a brow. "You know your dreams don't always come true."

"This one will." She put her hands over his. "How are they today?"

"Well enough," he said, lifting his hands and crossing his arms over his chest.

"That's excellent darling," she said brightly, avoiding his eyes.

"*Isabella.*"

"Hmm?" she murmured, moving away to needlessly reorganize the strawberry pots.

"You and I both know that they shouldn't be well—nowhere near. I just haven't figured out how you're doing it. The staff swears up and down that my meals and drink haven't been adulterated at your request. My valet swears the brandy and the grappa have not been tampered with. So, *mia streghetta*, how did you do it?"

Isobel pursed her lips and looked down.

"*Mi amore*, you have to stop."

She looked up at him entreatingly. "I can't."

He sat on the bench across from her and took her hands in his. "You have to. I told you—this is my penance. It's important to me. This is the only way to make amends for what I've done."

Scowling, she tugged on his glove. "And I've told you, there is no more need to punish yourself. You were a victim, just as I almost was. But you met me," she said, succeeding in pulling off the glove from his hand. "And our meeting was no accident. I know that now. I was supposed to help you and now I'm supposed to love you. So I'm going to do just that, and you will accept it—whether you like it or not."

He laughed briefly, until she lifted his hand to her lips to press a soft kiss to its scarred surface.

His eyes softened. "I happily accept your love and anything else you are willing to give me. Except the continued healing. I've already regained the use of my hands. Anything else is too much to ask. So please, no more charms or spells or whatever else it is that you've done."

She sighed. "I told you, I can't stop. But if you choose to forgo treatment, then that is your decision. I shall, however, be extremely disappointed. Although the natural conclusion of the treatment was fast approaching in any case," she said, patting her belly meaningfully.

He raised a brow. "What is that supposed to mean?"

She bit her lip and glanced at him from beneath her lashes. "It means that the charm is *in* me, my lord."

"What?"

Gesturing to her body, she suppressed a tiny gloating smile. "I put the healing charm in me. Every time you touch me, every time we make love, you are healed just a little bit more."

"Isabella!" he gasped, his eyes wide.

She held up her hands. "I didn't know I was pregnant when I cast the spell! I swear it! But even if had known I would have done it, anyway. In fact, I take comfort in the charm being there for all new reasons now," she said, casting worried eyes down her body.

Her husband wrapped his arms around her shoulders tightly. "Everything is going to be *fine*. No child of ours could be anything but good and pure, no matter when they were conceived."

Trying to be convincing, she agreed with him. It was an old argument between them.

Isobel wasn't sure when she'd fallen pregnant. It was most likely after Matteo had begun to recover from his ordeal, during one their first real lovemaking sessions. But there was the matter of her substitution in the contraceptive mixture of herbs she'd been taking before he was cured. And if her calculations were accurate, then there was a genuine possibility that the child had been conceived before the purge.

Clinging tighter to Matteo, she pressed her face into his neck, while he ran his hands over her back and bottom in a soothing gesture. His fingers flexed and lingered on the latter, as if he just couldn't help himself.

"You really are a witch, *mi amore*," he said.

Lifting her head, she met his teasing expression. "I think that's been suitably established my lord," she said wryly.

"I was referring to the healing charm you managed to imbue in your beautiful body. You picked the one thing I would never be able to deny myself," he said, gloved hands moving down her breasts to the apex of her thighs.

She blushed, growing warm beneath her dress. But her countenance was sober, because what she had to tell him was serious.

"It was still a risk, my lord. There was every chance that you'd grow tired of me now that you were alone in there," she said, pressing a hand to his chest.

He frowned and began to speak but she cut him off with a hand over his mouth.

"I was afraid, you see," she continued, moving her hand over his heart, "that your feelings for me were an artifact, a side-effect of your affliction. There was a danger that over time that your regard and those sentiments would fade away, as if they'd never been there. And if you didn't touch me, my cure would never work."

He laughed at her, and she scowled.

"It was a genuine concern."

He leaned in until their brows touched. "No, my love, there was never any danger of that at all," he whispered before he kissed her again.

And again. And again.

THE END.

AFTERWORD

Thank you for reading this novel! Reviews are an author's bread and butter. If you liked the story please consider leaving one.

Read the FREE short story The Hex, a Cursed Prequel

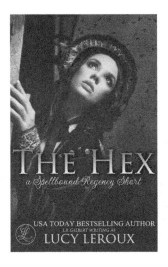

Available Now

Subscribe to the Lucy Leroux Newsletter for a *free* full-length novel!
www.authorlucyleroux.com/newsletter
or keep up with her L.B. Gilbert releases
www.elementalauthor.com/newsletter

NOTES ABOUT CURSED

First of all thank you for reading Cursed!

Some liberty has been taken with geographical details. The overall distances and how long it would take to travel them have been altered for the sake of brevity and convenience. Additionally to my knowledge there are no underground ruins of a fort in the town of Carrbridge. The bridge for which the town was named still exists, but the ruins are solely my creation. I would also like to add that I'm sure the inhabitants of the real Carrbridge are all lovely people who have never run a witch out of town.

I would also like to thank Alexandre Albore for all of his helpful suggestions on the historical accuracy of the characters. This includes changing the origin of the Garibaldi's from Varzi to Santa Fiora, in Tuscany so the rich Italian count could stay an Italian count, instead of a penniless french-speaking Marquess from Savoie!

Santa Fiora, unlike Varzi, is the ancestral home of a powerful dynasty of counts, though I chose not to use their family name, Aldobrandeschi, in favor of the more reader-friendly Garibaldi. Another big thanks to Alex for all of the translations. The swearing is far more accurate for Italians of this region as a result!

I'm also very aware that the incubus described differs from the historical accounts and mythology surrounding them. But hey, it's a fantasy ;)

CONTINUE THE SPELLBOUND SERIES WITH BLACK WIDOW

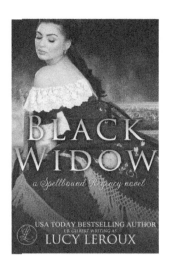

He wants to bring her to justice, but the secrets she holds may be the end of him.

Shattered by the death of his cousin, Gideon Wells, the Earl of Flint, is determined to prove that his widow is the one responsible. When Amelia Montgomery finally returns to town on the arm of her new lover, Gideon vows to bring her to justice. But getting close to her sparks a hunger that he can't ignore. As he begins to uncover the truth about Amelia, he encounters an evil more sinister than he ever imagined. Can he destroy the threat or will he suffer the same fate as his cousin?

Available Now

ABOUT THE AUTHOR

Lucy Leroux is another name for USA Today Bestselling Author L.B. Gilbert.

Seven years ago Lucy moved to France for a one-year research contract. Six months later she was living with a handsome Frenchman and is now married with an adorable half-french daughter.

When her last contract ended Lucy turned to writing. Frustrated by the lack of quality romance erotica she created her own.

Cursed is the first of many regency novels. Additionally, she writes two bestselling contemporary series. The 'Singular Obsession' books are a combination of steamy romance and suspense that feature intertwining characters in their own stand-alone stories. Follow her on twitter or facebook, or check our her website for more news!

www.authorlucyleroux.com

facebook.com/lucythenovelist
twitter.com/lucythenovelist
instagram.com/lucythenovelist

Made in the USA
Columbia, SC
27 May 2024

35916456R00114